Some
Sunny
Day

Books by Adam Baron

BOY UNDERWATER

YOU WON'T BELIEVE THIS

THIS WONDERFUL THING

SOME SUNNY DAY

ADAM BARON

HarperCollins *Children's Books*

First published in the United Kingdom by
HarperCollins *Children's Books* in 2022
HarperCollins *Children's Books*
is a division of HarperCollins*Publishers* Ltd
1 London Bridge Street
London SE1 9GF

www.harpercollins.co.uk

HarperCollins*Publishers*
1st Floor, Watermarque Building, Ringsend Road
Dublin 4, Ireland

1

ISBN 978-0-00-842237-0

A CIP catalogue record for this title is
available from the British Library.

Typeset in 11pt Sabon by Palimpsest Book Production Ltd,
Falkirk, Stirlingshire
Printed and bound in the UK using
100% renewable electricity at CPI Group (UK) Ltd

This book is produced from independently certified FSC™ paper
to ensure responsible forest management.

Find out more about HarperCollins and the environment at
www.harpercollins.co.uk/green

So many people, doing so many crucial jobs,
helped our children through lockdown.
Thanks to all of you.

This book, however, is for the teachers.

CHAPTER ONE

Here's something you won't believe. Not that long ago, I, Cymbeline Igloo, made two completely new BEST friends.

Why should you be surprised? This is lockdown we're talking about. No one was supposed to go near anyone else – let alone make friends with them. And my mum was totally paranoid – at least at the start.

'Social distancing' was like her catchphrase. If someone was walking towards us, she'd shout out 'STOP!' and 'WAIT THERE!' If people didn't hear, or just ignored her, we'd literally have to turn round and go the other way. Once, it took us half an hour to get to our corner shop! It was like being in a maze.

Another time there were people coming from both

directions – and neither were shifting over! I thought Mum would drag me into the road – but a bus was coming. So do you know what she did? Did she just walk past? Press us back as far as we could go?

No.

She told me to climb a tree!

She did! And she came after me. People pointed up at us like we were nuts, especially when she started shouting, 'TWO METRES! TWO METRES!' like some weird, enormous parrot. And the humiliation did NOT end there. We were up the tree for ages because joggers kept going by, and people in the flats opposite came onto their balconies and started filming us. We only escaped after one jogger was so surprised to see us up there that he tripped over a paving stone and went flying!

'Sorry!' Mum said (from the tree) as he was hobbling away.

As for my current two best friends, Mum wouldn't let me near them.

'It's not allowed,' she insisted, after we'd been in lockdown for what seemed like FOR EVER (about two weeks). I'd asked if I could see Lance. 'You can't meet up with anyone outside your own family.'

'But I don't want to meet up with him.'

'Then what do you want?'

'Are we allowed in Greenwich Park?'

'Of course.'

'And is Lance?'

'Yes. As long as . . .'

'Two metres. I know, I know. "So-cial dist-an-cing". So, what if you don't arrange with Lance's mum to meet in the park, but you tell her we'll be there? Then she could just HAPPEN to be there too. And if I HAPPEN to kick my football, then Lance, who would HAPPEN to be two metres away, could HAPPEN to kick it back!'

I was desperate for this to happen because I wanted to see how Lance was getting on with the lockdown football challenge that Mr Ashe (our teacher, and our football coach) had set us. But Mum wasn't having it. She said we could chat on Zoom instead, but it was rubbish. Lance just grunted 'All right?' and I grunted 'All right?' and that was it. We couldn't play anything. We couldn't do kick-ups. We couldn't do any Lego and there wasn't even any football to talk about because all the leagues were shut.

'I wonder what Jackie Chapman's doing now,' Lance said.

Jackie Chapman is the captain of Charlton Athletic Football Club, and our absolute HERO. I've got a club shirt that's signed by all the players, which Jackie Chapman ACTUALLY SENT ME. It's got my name on the back and when I thought burglars had nicked it last year, I nearly fainted. When I took it into school for Show and Tell, Mrs Stebbings came in for a look. She's our Chief Dinner Lady and loves Charlton EVEN MORE than Lance and I do. She stared at it like an angel had dropped it out of heaven.

'I don't know,' I said. 'But I know what Jackie Chapman's not doing.'

'What's that?'

'Hiding in trees,' I said. 'With his mum.'

We hung up after that because there was nothing else to say.

Our mums agreed that we should try again a few days later, and this time they both made us our favourite smoothie. That was pretty cool actually – until we tried to do a 'Cheers'. Lance went to touch his glass against his screen and he dropped it all over the keyboard. The last thing I saw was red goo running down the camera before the picture froze, went juddery, and then turned completely black.

'Let's try Veronique,' Mum said.

Veronique is my other best friend – but Zooming her was a disaster. First, we could hardly find a time to do it because Veronique was doing Zoom violin lessons and Zoom piano lessons. She was doing a Zoom orchestra too, and even Zoom fencing – though how you can whack someone with a sword online I have no idea. When we finally did manage to set up the call, it was actually fine – until Veronique started chatting about school.

'It's great,' she said. 'Isn't it?'

'Not being there? You bet.'

'No! Working online. Though not for everyone, of course. Imagine what it's like being Semira.'

I squinted. 'Semira?'

'You know! The *new* girl. As soon as she joined, we all got sent home. It must be really weird for her.'

'I suppose,' I said.

'Though for me, this is fabulous. I get so much more done!'

'You actually finish everything Mr Ashe puts on the online classroom?'

'That only takes half an hour. Then I do all the fun stuff. You know – BrainSqueeze Maths?'

'Er . . .'

'And Science-Solvers? IQ-English? That's great. You don't just get to read books – you get to write essays! They can be as long as you want!'

'*What*?' said Mum, from behind me.

Which was when Mum found out about all the 'enhancement activities' that Mr Ashe was putting up, and which she didn't exactly know about before because I may have, *accidentally,* deleted some of his emails from her iPad.

'Same time next week?' Veronique beamed.

'Er . . .'

'Fabulous!' Mum said. 'I'll send a link to your mum.'

I tried to shut our laptop but Mum grabbed hold of my hand.

'BrainSqueeze Maths,' she said. 'That does sound fun, doesn't it, Cymbeline Igloo? And two whole weeks to catch up on! Better get started, hadn't you?'

I sighed and did it, and thought about lockdown, and how Mum had said it was probably going to last for MONTHS. I was completely sure that WITHOUT friends, or Charlton, or Mrs Stebbings to talk to about Charlton, and WITH BrainSqueeze Maths, it was going to be the most excruciatingly BORING time that I'd ever had in my whole life.

But I was wrong.

Because of Wansa.

Though when I first laid eyes on Wansa, I was

FURIOUS.

CHAPTER TWO

It all started on a Sunday.

I know that because we normally have pancakes on Sunday mornings and I was SO looking forward to them. When I came downstairs to the kitchen however, I got a shock.

The Weetabix were out on the table.

'Mum!' I said.

'What?'

I sighed. Mum was rooting around in the cupboard below the sink. I put my hand on her back. 'I know all the days seem the same at the moment,' I said, trying not to sound too annoyed. 'But it's SUNday.'

'So?'

'Er, flat things? Used for the delivery of chocolate spread to my stomach?'

'Ah.' Mum stood up and plonked a bottle of bleach on the counter. 'Sorry. I haven't got any flour.'

'What? So, no pancakes? This, after you made me eat fish fingers last night WITH NO TOMATO KETCHUP?'

'Well, I'm sorry. It's the shops. They've run out of things. Because of Covid. We saw it on the news last night, remember?'

I did remember. Mum watched the news all the time, looking for the numbers of people who had Covid, and how fast it was spreading. 'Yes, but . . .'

'Anyway, I'm too busy.'

'On Sunday? In *lockdown*?! What can you possibly be doing?'

'Cleaning!' Mum said.

With that, Mum pulled on a pair of squeaky yellow gloves and knelt down to scrub the floor. I frowned. I couldn't see anything wrong with the floor. It looked like a . . . floor. Mum didn't rest until it looked more like an ice rink, though, while I spooned the last of the chocolate spread onto some Weetabix and tried to ignore the smell of bleach.

The kitchen cupboards were next. They seemed fine to me too, but I watched as Mum REALLY went at them, her nose wrinkling up as she did these fast little circles with the sponge. She even unscrewed the handles to clean underneath them – and she did the drawers too. And not just the outsides! I stared as she got the contents out – knives and forks, plates and pans all piled up on the counter.

'What's the point?' I asked, after finishing my second Weetabix. 'Cupboards are normally shut!'

But Mum didn't listen. And she even made me help! On a SUNDAY! I nearly phoned the police. While she cleaned the insides of the cupboards, I had to sort everything out, ready to be put back in. Quite a lot of the stuff was old, though, like chipped mugs that we didn't use, or pans with wobbly handles. Mum squinted at them, then knelt up straighter.

'Right then,' she said.

Which meant, apparently, that we were going to have a 'Clear Out'. Mum was SO excited, which I couldn't get my head round. I'm excited when I *get* things, not when I chuck them away. Was it her way of dealing with what we were going through?

And it wasn't just lockdown, actually, that *she* was

going through. Mum got engaged last year – to Stephan. He moved in next door with his daughters, Ellen and Mabel, and he and Mum were supposed to be getting married soon. There was only one problem. Stephan went back to New Zealand with his daughters just before lockdown began. Now – thanks to Covid-19 – he couldn't get back.

At first I wasn't sure about him. My dad had come back into our lives when Stephan and Mum first met. Like most kids, I suppose, I wanted my mum and dad to get back together – or for nothing to happen, for Mum and I to go on being like we were. Just her and me. Mum told me that she wasn't getting back with Dad, though, and then I got to know Stephan. And he was great. I also came to appreciate my soon-to-be stepsisters, in spite of the fact that Ellen was a bit jealous of me and Mabel drew unicorn horns on all my Charlton posters. I was looking forward to it all, though not as much as Mum was, of course.

She was clearly missing Stephan, but did that explain this odd desire to clean things and chuck stuff out? I didn't know, and rather than try to understand The Strange Ways of Adults, I went through to the living room to hit our Seated Optimal Flop-out

Activator (S.O.F.A.) for some well-deserved TV-ME time. But Mum called me straight back through! I growled and stomped back, remembering a conversation I'd had with Lance, before lockdown began.

'Thing is,' Lance had said. 'You can't let parents make it seem like helping is normal.'

'Like something we actually should be doing?'

'Exactly! If you help once, without complaining, they'll just get you to help again!'

'Will they? That's terrible. So, you've got to complain about it *every* time?'

'Absolutely! When my dad says, 'Lance, can you clear the table please?' I say, 'But I cleared the table yesterday!'

'What if you didn't clear the table yesterday?'

'I never admit that! He doesn't remember. I still complain, and when the drying up needs doing, he stares at it. He still wants me to do it but, if I've complained properly before, he just shakes his head and does it himself. Do you see?'

I did see, and I put on my TOTALLY NOT HAPPY face, getting ready to go to PEAK COMPLAIN as I marched back through to Mum. But Mum was smiling at me, her eyes moist like she might start crying.

'Cym,' she said, in a voice that was about right for talking to a toddler. 'Look what I found!'

Mum was back on the floor, kneeling next to a big cardboard box. It already had quite a few pans in, as well as lots of plastic plates that she'd bunched up with rubber bands.

'Won't Mabel need those?' I asked.

Mum shook her head. 'She's old enough for real ones now. But I don't mean those. Look at this!'

Mum reached into the box, and I laughed. She was holding a two-handled beaker – with Thomas the Tank Engine on the front! I used to LOVE Thomas the Tank Engine. I'd had a plate as well, not to mention about a million books and a whole train track. Thomas the Tank Engine was my whole world and now I never even thought about him. It was weird, and after Mum dropped the beaker back into the box, I whipped it out again and put it back in the cupboard without her seeing. Then I had a thought.

'This "Clear Out",' I said.

'What about it?'

'You're JUST doing the kitchen, right?'

'Oh no,' Mum said. 'With all this time on our hands? I'm going to . . .'

But I did NOT listen. I sprinted back into the living room and flung myself against the toy cupboard.

'You're not touching it!' I shouted.

Mum came through, the yellow gloves making her look VERY menacing. 'What? Half that stuff, you never play with any more.'

'I do!'

'All right,' Mum insisted. 'Tell me what's in there.'

'Games,' I said. 'And . . . toys.'

'What toys?'

'It doesn't matter! They're my toys. And you're not clearing them out!'

Mum held her yellow hands up. 'What about books, then?'

'YOU ARE NOT TOUCHING MY CHARLTON ANNUALS. I'LL TELL MRS STEBBINGS!'

'Of course not. But what about picture books?'

I thought about it. '*Where the Wild Things Are* stays.'

'Deal,' Mum said. 'What else?'

We kept about half in the end (because of Mabel) including *The Pencil*, *The Mousehole Cat*, *The Gruffalo*, *Alfie* and *Mack and the Big Truck*. When we came across a big Winnie the Pooh book, Mum couldn't resist reading some of the poems.

'You're so like Pooh,' Mum said.

'Me? I don't even like honey.'

'If Pooh was obsessed with chocolate spread.'

'Rubbish. Anyway, I'm glad I'm not *him*.'

I pointed down to that poem about James James, Whatsit Whatsit, who lost his mum when he was three. My mum smiled quickly and put the book in the 'Keep' pile.

She did the cupboard under the stairs after that – and did that toddler voice again. She'd found the seat I used to have to sit on, on the loo.

'You used to look so cute on that!'

'What? Doing a poo?'

Mum said yes, actually, I did. Apparently, my 'little legs' used to stick out and wiggle. I sighed, and we did the shed. We carried the boxes out to the street where Mum squirted them with Dettol. She made a sign – *Covid-free. Please Take!* – and looked pleased with herself, while I just stared down at all the junk we'd cleared out. I was puzzled to realise that none of it seemed like ours any more.

It was just *stuff*.

'Right,' I said. 'Can you make some pancakes *now*?'

'I told you, we've no flour.'

'Make them without, then.'

'Not possible.'

'Well, can't you go and buy some more?'

'I've told you, the shops have run out. Anyway, we're not finished.'

'Aren't we?' I frowned. 'What else is there to do?'

'Well.' Mum narrowed her eyes. 'I thought . . .'

'You thought what?'

'That we might just have a teensy, weensy go at . . .

'Your bedroom?'

'No.'

'Then . . . ?'

'Not *my* bedroom . . .'

'WHAT?!'

I was back inside and up the stairs like a SHOT. I shoved my door shut behind me and barricaded it with a chair.

'Cym?' She was right behind the door. The Yellow-Handed Clear-Out Fiend.

'You're not coming in!' I screamed.

'But Cym . . .'

'ENTRY REFUSED!'

'Cymbeline! You don't even know what I'm . . .'

'You're NOT having my Subbuteo!'

'I don't want it.'

'OR my Match Attax.'

'Those card things? That get everywhere? If you insist. But what about all those plastic medals you get just for going to birthday parties at that football place? And those cardboard trains? You made them in Reception. They're lovely and everything but . . .'

'They're staying!'

'But . . .'

'EAR MALFUNCTION! EAR MALFUNCTION!'

'Okay. Okay! You'll take it all to university with you, I get it. But how about . . . ?'

'What?'

'Clothes?' Mum said.

I hesitated, and Mum sensed it.

'Your drawers are stuffed, Cym. You've really grown in the last six months. And Mabel's not going to want any of your old pants, is she?'

I wasn't sure about that, because Mabel REALLY likes me. But what did I care about clothes? This clear-out thing was obviously making Mum happy. It was so much better for her than staring at the news and getting anxious. So I pulled the chair back from the door and opened it a bit.

'ONLY clothes?'

I peered through the crack, and saw Mum nod. 'Yes.'

'Promise?'

'Absolutely.'

'Say it, then.'

Mum frowned. 'What?'

'Promise.'

'Oh. Okay. I, Janice Igloo, do solemnly swear . . .'

'Wait!' I said. 'Get your phone out so we can record it.'

Mum raised her eyes, but did, hereby promising not to take anything other than clothes out of my bedroom, so help her God.

'Don't you want to do it with me?' she asked, after I'd let her in.

'Pants-sorting? Nah,' I said. 'Have all the fun you want. GO for it.'

And I left her there, figuring that yes, all this extreme cleaning and clearing out must be her way of coping with being stuck at home all the time, and the worry about catching Covid-19. I went downstairs to FINALLY hit the Seated Optimal Flop-out Activator (S.O.F.A.) for some well-deserved TV-ME time.

Which, as I found out THE VERY NEXT MORNING, was a

MASSIVE

MiSTAKE.

CHAPTER THREE

'Cym?' Mum said (THE NEXT MORNING).

I didn't answer.

'Cym?' she repeated, and again I stayed silent, which you probably think is a bit rude. I wasn't being rude, though, I promise. What I was being, was asleep. And not a little bit asleep, like I am when she normally wakes me up. I was A LOT asleep. I had no idea what the time actually was, but I knew that it was nowhere near getting-up time. Mum, however, refused to be ignored.

'Cym,' she insisted. 'I've had the most wonderful idea!'

With that, Mum joggled my shoulder. When that had no effect on me, she DELIBERATELY committed one of the most serious of Parental Sins: she yanked my duvet off! Then she pulled me to my feet. She led me into the bathroom, where I finally opened my eyes properly. I happened to be staring at the wall clock which, I assumed, must have stopped.

Because it said 5.15 a.m.!

But it hadn't stopped.

'We'll have the park to ourselves!' Mum explained. 'We won't have to worry about other people! Why didn't I think of this before?'

Once my incredibly sleepy brain had processed this information, I yawned at her. 'Because it's the middle of the night?'

'Don't be silly, Cym. Look, we're allowed out once a day. Everyone else is going to be out later. Why do the same as them?'

The answer to that was that everyone else was SENSIBLE. I didn't say it, though. There was no point. Mum was set on it, and all I could do was let her grab my arms and legs and shove some clothes on me. Then she led me downstairs.

'Breakfast now?' she asked. 'Or later?'

'Later.' I rubbed my eyes. *Now* isn't even today. We should be having supper, if anything. It's still yesterday.'

But Mum wouldn't listen. She jammed some

trainers onto my feet and a football into my arms, before picking up her bag. Then she unlocked the front door.

And it was WEIRD.

I was still half asleep and, for a second, I thought I'd walked out of a different house. I mean, I know my street – I see it every day – but it was different. The light was very new, covering everything like fresh paint. It made things stand out – the parked cars, for instance, which all seemed very separate from each other. And heavy. The curbs, the black windows of the flats opposite. And the street smelled different – all fresh and clean – and it sounded different too. There were no voices or car horns, just the sparrows who were being really noisy in the trees across the road. There was a rumble in the distance – a train coming into Lewisham, which we don't normally hear because of the traffic.

Then I noticed the shadows.

Our house was casting a big shadow onto the pavement that was as black and solid-looking as the bricks themselves. Other shadows – all the way down the road – were so long and thin that they looked like prison bars, until I realised that they came from the iron railings by the side of the road. They stretched down to the corner – where something was moving.

It was a fox, nosing at a wheelie bin on the pavement. You see foxes quite a lot in London but I'd never seen one like this. Maybe it was just because the street was empty but it looked MASSIVE, and totally wild, with a big scar across its black muzzle. I realised that I normally thought of London foxes as living in our world, but this was definitely *its* world. Mum and I didn't really belong there and I had this sense of there being nothing at all between its teeth and me. When it turned its head and stared at us, I froze.

'Wow,' Mum whispered, and I just nodded, my eyes wide, until the fox disappeared up the alleyway towards the main road.

I stood for a minute and blinked. It was amazing – as if the world I knew, and was comfortable in, had another world that lived just beneath it.

But the street was nothing compared to the park.

I thought Mum would take me to Greenwich Park. She told me it wouldn't be open yet, though, so we turned the corner towards Lewisham instead. A huge yawn seemed to crack me open, my body waking up now in spite of itself. I blinked at the wheelie bins, standing on the empty pavement like guards on sentry. Then I noticed the cats. There were loads of them, eyeing us from windowsills as we walked past, or from the tops of the garden walls. I turned from them to the windows of the houses and flats, a bit freaked out to think of all the people just behind them, sleeping. They were actually really close to us, and we crept past them like burglars – until a soft whirring sounded from up ahead. It was a milk float. Mum waved her arms until the float stopped, which I thought was odd because she really did want to avoid people. From a very safe distance, though, she spoke to the driver about getting some milk delivered to our house. He smiled at me from behind his face mask.

'You're supposed to book it online,' he said. 'Though I know that's tricky at the mo.'

'That's all right,' Mum said, stepping back behind me. 'I understand.'

The man laughed quietly, though, and said he'd sort us out. Mum said thanks SO much and gave him our address, and then we watched the float go on again, the whirring accompanied by the gentle tinkling of milk bottles, like sleigh bells.

'Come on,' Mum said, and she took my hand as we crossed over the road, which seemed much longer than it normally did, probably because there were no cars coming and I could see further down it.

Then we got to the DLR station (Docklands Light Railway).

Mulberry Park is on the other side of it. It's not a big park but it's got a pond, lots of trees, a little playground, and something that – quite literally – took our breath away.

There's a footbridge over the DLR track, just next to some allotments (I'll talk about them later). We climbed up to the bridge, and I hesitated. Mum normally pretends to be a troll while I run past, but we both had the sense that it was too quiet for that. Instead, we held hands, Mum wincing when our footsteps clanged on the metal stairs going down. They echoed a bit at the bottom, but no one seemed to hear, so we walked on again. I was about to drop the football so we could play but – suddenly – Mum's hand tightened.

And I saw the river.

The river is called the Ravensbourne. It flows alongside the edge of Mulberry Park into the Thames. I've seen it loads of times. It's got bushes and trees on the high banks that go down to it, some of which go underwater when the tide from the Thames is high. Sometimes it's got old footballs in the water, or shopping trolleys, and there are usually a few plastic bags stuck in the reeds along the banks. It's a really normal city river, though it was anything but normal today.

Because of the mist.

The whole top of the river was white. The mist was about five feet tall, completely covering the water as it wound through the park. And the mist was moving! It was like a giant white snake, slithering through the city while all the people were sleeping. I was mesmerised, first by this magical thing, happening in our normal park, so close to where I live. Then I thought back to the sleeping people. I was stunned to think that all around us were thousands of them, millions even, but only Mum and I, out of all of them, were here.

Though I was wrong.

Mum dropped my hand and moved forward. There's a low wall at the top of the steep riverbank and she sat on it, even though it looked a bit damp. Keeping her eyes on the mist-creature, she used her right hand to search in her bag. It came out with an ink pen and a sketch pad, which she flipped open while pulling the lid off the pen with her teeth. Mum's an artist (and an art teacher) and she gets like this – totally absorbed, caught by something that just has to be sketched. I watched as the mist appeared again, this time on her pad, though there's only so much sketch-watching that you can do. I didn't want to disturb Mum, though, so I didn't ask her to come and have a kickaround with me. Instead I told her where I'd be – on the flat bit further on, near the little playground.

Mum said that was fine and she wouldn't be long, though I didn't mind if she was. Lockdown was being hard on her. I knew how much she missed Stephan – and how much she worried about me. It was great to see her doing something she really wanted to, even if it was before the day had actually begun.

And she's rubbish at football anyway.

I mean, SOOOOOO rubbish.

I left Mum and wandered on, with the river on my right. The mist seemed to be speeding up a bit and I put the ball on the floor and started to dribble it, trying to keep up. I did a few stepovers, and a 360 that didn't quite work, and I got to the flat place in no time. And it was as weird as my street. Most of the flat bit was in shadow – because of the trees. Fingers of light were pushing through them, though, like Mum's fingers sometimes do in my hair. They lit up small patches of the grass, each blade shining with dewdrops. I turned from them to the little playground, which was taped shut because of the virus. The swings and seesaw were dead still, as if the White Witch in Narnia had got to them first. It was a bit eerie and I looked away, concentrating on my football instead. I did a few kick-ups, the thump of the ball sounding really loud when I messed up and it landed on the grass.

It was odd, then.

Perhaps it was because it was so quiet. And still. But I started to do kick-ups REALLY well! I even drew with my Personal Best – which made me think of Mr Ashe's lockdown challenge. It's called the Super Seven and it's IMPOSSIBLE. First you have to do two normal kick-ups, using both feet (hard enough on its own). These are then followed by two knee-ups, followed by two shoulder-ups, and then a header!

All without the ball hitting the ground!

Three goes in our garden had told me that I would never do it in a million years – but that was in the normal world. What about in this strange morning-world? I kicked the ball up with my right foot, then had a go with my left. I normally avoid my left foot – but the ball went up again. It went up onto my left knee, and then onto my right. From there it went up again – almost on its own – to my shoulders. I'd never even tried ONE shoulder-up before, let alone TWO, but I did both, with these lopsided shrugs.

And they worked!

The ball went straight as a pencil until, with a very loud BONK, it came back down.

On my head!

SEVEN!

I squealed, pumping my fist like crazy. I'd hardly ever been so excited – until I thought of something. Mr Ashe had told us to film ourselves and put the videos up in the Chat Room. But how could I? There was no way I'd ever be able to do this again, let alone on film, and no one had been here to witness it. I was about to howl in frustration, but then I had a thought. Mum: had she finished her sketch? Had she seen me after all? I spun back towards the way I'd come, along the grey path that wound its way through the sparkly grass.

But it was empty.

Mum hadn't come and I was crushed – but then I stopped. I was getting a feeling: a strange, twitchy sort of feeling. And it was growing. I even shivered. I didn't understand why at first, but suddenly I did – and I froze. And then I turned my head round slowly, completely and utterly certain about what the feeling meant.

SOmeOne was watching me.

CHAPTER FOUR

He was down by the edge of the riverbank.

A kid.

The reason I could see him was because the mist-snake had started to shed its skin – by which I mean that it was beginning to break up. The magic of this early-morning time was beginning to wear off.

The kid was thin. He was about my age, with a baseball cap backwards on his head. I'd probably noticed him because of his shirt, though: it was bright red. I stared at it for a moment before turning away, hoping the kid hadn't seen how scared I'd been. That made me feel a bit stupid and I was about to run off to find Mum, but I stopped and looked back at the kid, because of the shirt. It was a football shirt. The red colour meant it was probably Liverpool or Arsenal but the team didn't matter; if someone had a football shirt on, then they almost definitely *liked football*.

Which meant that they might want a quick kickaround.

Before Mum came!

Yes!

The idea of booting a ball about with someone else was brilliant, so, forcing myself to get over my embarrassment, I took a couple of steps forward.

'Hello!' I hissed, so Mum wouldn't hear.

Before the kid could answer, though, the mist closed up – and the kid vanished. Hoping to see through it, I ran forward, up to the little wall at the top of the bank. I squinted at the running mist until another gap appeared. This gap was a bit further along but, yes, I could see the kid again. He was moving away, though, so I called out again. When he didn't stop, I figured that he couldn't have heard me. I followed, keeping on the path at the top of the bank, with him down below. He was swallowed again but then he reappeared, as another hole opened in the snake. This one was bigger than the last one, though it was still pretty grey and not quite as clear.

'Hello!' I called. 'You down there!'

And it was weird. The kid MUST have heard me. I'd been much louder this time – but he went faster, if anything, moving towards the far end of the park. It was almost like he was afraid of me, and I frowned, about to leave it. If he didn't want to play, what could I do? But I thought of something. What if the kid had been there for a while?

What if he'd seen me doing the Super Seven?!

I could get him to write a witness statement! It would be proof! I could show it to Lance, and to Mr Ashe!

I called out once more but again I got no response – the kid just picked his way through the bushes at the water's edge. Then he climbed over a fallen branch – which is when I got a better look at him. And his shirt.

No, it wasn't Liverpool. Or Arsenal. The badge on the sleeve was wrong. Was it Man U, then? I thought *maybe*, but no, that's got a devil on it, and this . . . ? I squinted. This badge had a black and red circle with a hand in the middle, gripping a white sword.

Blimey!

The kid was wearing a Charlton shirt!

Did he LOVE Jackie Chapman too?

I simply couldn't believe it. This gave me an even bigger reason to stop the kid. I shouted out yet again, wanting him to turn so that I could tell him that I SUPPORT CHARLTON AS WELL! Surely he'd want a kickaround now! And he'd write me a note. But the kid only glanced back at me before darting off again – showing me the back of his shirt properly.

Now, when you buy a football shirt, you don't HAVE to get a name put on the back of it. You can leave it blank. Most people do get a name, though, and the kid's shirt had one. Was it Chapman? I squinted. No, it looked shorter. March, then? He plays for Charlton too and he's a legend. But it wasn't that, either; it was something I could just make out before the mist-snake closed up again, swallowing the kid for a final time as I came to a crunching halt.

And a hand seemed to grab my throat.

Because of the name.

Which I saw as surely as I've ever seen ANYTHING.

And it was?

IGLOO

CHAPTER FIVE

'MUM!'

I bellowed.

CHAPTER SIX

I've actually MET Jackie Chapman.

It's true. In fact, he and I once went on an adventure. Afterwards, he gave me some home-game tickets. I took Lance and it was great, though Mum told me not to expect anything else after that. I didn't; I was content with the memory and the ticket stubs, which I kept in a special box (I showed that to Mrs Stebbings, too). But, one Saturday morning, the postman arrived with a package. I assumed it was for Mum because I never got packages, but it had MY name on. I took it in and gawped at it like Charlie Bucket did with his golden ticket: but there wasn't chocolate inside. There was something even better.

A brand-new, gleaming, signed-by-ALL-the-players Charlton shirt.

I couldn't believe it! My hero – someone who I screamed out for in the stand along with thousands and thousands of others – had sent me this shirt. It was like a spotlight shining on me, but the joy didn't stop there. After reading every single signature, I finally thought to turn the shirt over – and what I saw was amazing.

My name.

Jackie Chapman hadn't just sent me a signed shirt, he'd got it printed for me! I stared at it until Mum told me to try it on. I did, though that was the last time I ever wore it. It was WAY too precious. We were in the kitchen and I ran straight out, in case it got food on it. I took it off and then went back to get the oven gloves. Veronique's dad collects stamps, and he NEVER touches them. I put the gloves on and folded the shirt up (with difficulty) and then asked Mum to get it framed (preferably with bullet-proof glass). When it was done, I took it into school for Show and Tell and after that it lived at home, on my bedroom wall, where I showed it off to only the most honoured of guests, and then only if they promised to keep well back. It stayed there until some burglars broke in. They didn't steal it but they did smash the glass. Mum promised to get it framed again, but lockdown came so she couldn't.

And ever since then . . .

IT HAD LIVED WITH THE REST OF MY CLOTHES!

'Cymbeline?' Mum said, after sprinting up from the other end of the park.

Mum was wide-eyed because of my screaming. But I didn't answer her. I ran along the top of the riverbank – and stared down towards the water. I told myself NOT to panic. I knew this park. The kid had gone on towards the far end of it but there's a bridge there. He wouldn't be able to go any further. He'd have to come along the bank towards me, or else turn back the way he'd come. Either way, I'd be able to see him because the mist really was breaking up. It was no longer a snake, but now clumps of grey like dirty dishcloths.

'Cymbeline?' repeated Mum.

I didn't answer. I needed to find this kid so Mum could explain. She could tell him what had happened – my shirt had gone out *by mistake*. Mum hadn't meant to give it away. She'd MAKE the kid give the shirt back to me. It should have been easy to find him now, because even though some of the mist balls were still pretty thick, they were moving.

But he was nowhere to be seen!

It was like some magician had made him vanish. So, had I missed him? Had he slipped past me?

He couldn't have done.

So where WAS he?

In total confusion, I sprinted to the end of the park. I shot out through the iron gates and stared up the road, which was empty but for a solitary bus, lumbering off from a stop. I glared after it as Mum caught up with me again, asking, 'What's going on?' I just ran back into the park and all the way along to the DLR station, and the allotments.

And then I legged it home.

I sprinted ALL the way, Mum trailing after me, still demanding explanations until I was pointing at our front door.

'Unlock it!' I panted.

Mum did. And I sprinted upstairs, and hope burst into my chest: there was another kid called Igloo. As unusual as my name is, there was another kid who had it – and he was a Charlton fan too! I shoved my bedroom door open and slid down on my knees – to my shirts drawer. I pulled it open, shocked for a moment by just how tidy mum had left my clothes – not that I cared. I grabbed some school shirts and flung them behind me. I grabbed my St Saviour's football shirt and flung that too, as well as a posh shirt that Mum had got me for Auntie Mill's 'significant' birthday. Then I grabbed all my other shirts, desperate to see a folded piece of red – but all I could see was the faded old newspaper that lined the bottom of the drawer.

The EMPTY drawer.

CHAPTER SEVEN

'Cym?' Mum said, for the fourth time, as she knelt down right beside me. 'What's the matter?'

I told Mum what she'd done and the colour drained from her face. She *tried* to apologise.

'Oh no,' she whispered. 'It must have got caught up in some other stuff. I can't have seen it. Oh, Cym, I don't know what to . . .'

But I did not listen. Mum had put my most prized possession in the UNIVERSE outside the door – with a box of broken pans and a bag of old Thomas the Tank Engine pants. That fact was so huge that I could hardly hear what Mum was saying, though I could vaguely tell that she was going on about the frame getting smashed.

'You should have got it fixed!' I screamed.

'But I couldn't,' she pleaded. 'The framer's shut because of lockdown. Listen.'

'What?'

'I'll . . . write to Jackie Chapman.'

'What for?'

'I'll ask him to send a replacement.'

'But how CAN he?'

'Well . . .'

'He's not even THERE! He's at his house. And how could he get the other players to sign it? They're all at their houses. Brett Casey doesn't even play for Charlton now. He's gone to Wycombe Wanderers. I was really upset when he left but AT LEAST I HAD HIS SIGNATURE ON MY SHIRT!'

'Cym . . .'

'That shirt is unique!' I screamed. 'It was given to me by Jackie Chapman! He did it without being asked. It's the only one in the entire WORLD and you CLEARED IT OUT! So, unless you can UN-CLEAR IT OUT, why don't you

LEAVE

ME

ALONE?'

Which Mum did.

She tried to think of something else to say, but nothing would come. So, after taking a big, deep breath, she walked out of the room. She immediately turned and looked back at me, once again searching for words, until I marched over to the door.

And SLAMMED it in her face.

There was silence, then. After that came Mum's footsteps, first turning round, then going down the stairs. I heard each one, wondering when they'd stop. They had to, because she had to come back. She had SO not apologised enough, especially as I thought of another thing. What if I happened to run into Jackie Chapman? And what if he asked about my shirt? It would be so embarrassing. What could I say? 'Oh, that. Mum put it out on the street!' I needed to make Mum aware of that, but the footsteps carried on down the stairs and into the kitchen.

I put my hands on my hips and shook my head. Was Mum just going to get on with things? Was she going to make herself a nice cup of tea? Would she text Auntie Mill about some trivial thing? Did she not understand what I was going through? I hissed to myself and then did the only thing that I COULD do in such a terrible circumstance.

I stomped.

Our house is really good for stomping. It's old, and if you really put your feet into it, the lampshade in the kitchen wobbles. (I know this because Lance and I experimented.) And today I did not hold back. First, I stomped over to the bookcase in the far corner.

Four stomps.

Then I stomped back again.

Another four stomps.

After that I stomped to my bed (three stomps), and after that, I stomped over to the wall where my Charlton shirt USED to live (five stomps). Then I just stomped generally (stomp, stomp, stomp, stomp, stomp, stomp, stomp, stomp, stomp, stomp) which I knew Mum could NOT ignore. She MUST have heard me, and I was expecting her to run up the stairs and order me to 'STOP STOMPING!', which would give me another chance to scream at her about what an unforgivable thing she'd done.

But there were no footsteps.

I frowned. Mum *had* to come back up. She had to COMPLETELY understand how I felt, which she could only do by me bellowing at her. I stomped a bit more but she still didn't appear and I frowned. Should I slam the door again? No. It was shut, and it would be really obvious that I'd just opened it again so that I could slam it. I was left with only one option, an even more extreme action than stomping.

Which was crying.

Mum can NEVER resist it when I cry. She can be as mad at me as anything but, if I cry, she's like cheese under the grill. She goes all melty. So, I did it then, knowing, of course, that as soon as her face appeared round the bedroom door – looking all worried – I could stop the crying and shout at her again.

But I don't think she could hear me.

I opened the door. I carried on crying, but still no Mum. That made me cross, so I humphed and marched to the top of the stairs, about to start crying AGAIN. But I could hear something – coming from the kitchen. I didn't understand it at first – until I realised.

There was no point me crying.

No point at all.

Crying was already happening.

CHAPTER EIGHT

I crept to the bottom of the stairs and peered round the banister. Mum was sitting at the kitchen table. She was on the phone and I thought she was talking to Auntie Mill. It was still too early, though – so it had to be Stephan. He's in New Zealand, which is ten hours ahead, and they often FaceTimed each other in our morning. These FaceTimes used to be okay. They'd say how much they missed each other and go a bit gooey, but then Stephan had had to tell Mum that Covid-19 meant that he and the girls were stuck in New Zealand. Mum had cried, then, and she was crying again, now.

Mum was crying and trying to speak at the same time. That made me cross. Yes, Mum missed Stephan, but he hadn't vanished for ever, had he? He would be back! I'd just lost my Charlton shirt, which I would NEVER SEE AGAIN! I was about to stomp down the stairs and tell her that – but I stopped.

And felt a sort of stomp inside my chest.

Because Mum was talking about me.

'It was so special to him.' The words came out in little gaspy parcels. 'And. I. Lost. It. All because I can't relax. I'm in this frenzy all the time, to DO things. Why can't I slow down? Why can't I just accept it all, Stephan?'

I couldn't hear Stephan's reply because of Mum's crying – but I did know this: Mum does EVERYTHING for me. Seeing her face when she found things from my past had reminded me of that. She'd made a mistake with my shirt – TRUE – but it's not like she meant to. And the fact that she was SO upset scared me. Mum's had problems in the past, with her health. Her mental health. She even had to go into hospital once. So, to hear her crying now, stopped me – because it sounded sort of similar to how she'd sounded that time.

What if it happened again?

The anger inside me vanished. Just like that mist had. Yes, I still wanted my shirt back, but there was something that I wanted far more – Mum. So, without thinking, I pulled myself round the banister and ran downstairs. I sprinted into the kitchen, piling onto Mum's lap before she knew what I was doing. She looked at me, shocked, trying to get herself together, trying to pretend that she hadn't been crying. I ignored that and flung my arms round her neck, giving her the tightest hug I could.

'It's okay,' I insisted. 'He's rubbish anyway.'

'Who is?'

'Brett Casey. He doesn't track. Wycombe are welcome to him. It doesn't matter, okay?'

'Oh, Cymbeline.'

Mum looked at me as a big laugh bucked up from inside her. Another one came and then she cried a bit more, and then laughed, and then cried, and all the while I could see a face, looking up at us from the screen of Mum's phone, which was propped up against the Weetabix box.

'Hello, Stephan,' I said.

CHAPTER NINE

Mum went off to wash her face. I picked Stephan up (well, the phone) and he asked how I was. I started to answer, but Mabel came onto the screen, wearing a pair of unicorn pyjamas. She's the youngest of his two daughters and she can never quite get my name quite right.

'Thimbeline!' she said.

I waved at Mabel and then had to listen as she babbled on about all the things she'd been doing in New Zealand. I didn't interrupt but I knew she must be making most of them up. The park? A mountain walk? We were in lockdown! I just raised my eyes, until she asked what was quite a difficult question.

'Are you missing us, Thimbeline?'

For a second, I didn't answer. I mean, I did really like them all, but since they'd been gone I'd had some space to myself – for a change – and that had been quite nice. Though I didn't admit this to Mum. She missed them all SO much. But Mabel, who was supposed to live next door, was in our house ALL the time. She drew me a unicorn picture EVERY SINGLE DAY, insisting that I put it up on my bedroom wall. Lance thought it was hilarious. When they left, I took them down and shoved them under my bed. I had to admit, though, that the house did seem a bit too quiet now.

I said I was missing them, and then Stephan asked what I'd been doing.

'Er, nothing,' I replied. 'That's the point of lockdown, I think.'

He laughed. 'Not even Subbuteo?' Subbuteo is a football game with little plastic players and Stephan knows I LOVE it.

'Who with?' I asked.

'Your mum?'

'What? She's hopeless.'

'Thanks!' Mum said, from behind me.

'I mean, she's learning. But she can't play anyway.'

'Why not?'

'She's been banned. She knelt on two of my players and snapped their heads off. Violent conduct. She's got to miss the next three games.'

'Then how are the kick-ups coming along?'

'Good.' I told Stephan about the park, and how I hadn't got any proof.

'Shame,' he sighed. 'But I'm sure your teacher will believe you. How's the rest of school going?'

I pretended to strangle myself.

'It can't be that bad! What about science?'

'Boring. We're not doing any experiments.'

'Can't you do some at home?'

'Mr Ashe told us to put a Mentos mint in a bottle of Diet Coke. Apparently, it explodes.'

'That sounds like fun!'

'But Mum won't buy the Diet Coke because of the plastic bottle. She's gone more environmental than that Greta Iceberg.'

For some reason, Stephan laughed again. 'What about history? Time you had a new project, isn't it?'

Now that was a good point. We'd been doing Henry VIII but that had been cut off because of lockdown (like his wives' heads). Mr Ashe had said he was going to post our new project soon and I wanted to go online and find out what it was. But Stephan asked me to wait.

'Listen,' he said, from the screen. 'Your mum told me about your shirt. I'm really sorry. But I also just saw how nice you were about it. That means you'll find it.'

I frowned. 'Because I hugged Mum?'

'There's a saying: what goes around comes around. So have faith – and come up with a plan.'

'Right,' I said, though I didn't believe him. What plan could I think of for seeing that kid again? I just shrugged and we said goodbye, after which Mum went on the online classroom.

And we saw that Stephan was right.

Mr Ashe had put the project up. Mum clicked on the link and I blinked at pictures of aeroplanes and ships, and searchlights cutting through the sky.

'Is that . . . ?'

'Yes,' Mum said. 'You're doing World War Two.'

'Fantastic!'

I was well psyched. We were going to do the Battle of Britain and D-Day. It sounded great, though when I read on, I realised that that was all going to be after half term. First, there was this other stuff.

'The Home Front,' I said, squinting at the screen. 'What even is that?'

'Oh.' Mum nodded. 'It's about civilians. The people at home.'

'Not the soldiers, then?'

'Well, not to start with.'

'Great. How thrilling.'

'It will be,' Mum insisted. 'You'll learn about how the war affected home life. Rationing, for example.'

'I already know about that. We're out of chocolate spread *and* ketchup. Those fish fingers last night were disgusting.'

'They were the same fish fingers that I always get!'

'With no tomato ketchup! So they tasted like fish! I know about rationing. I'm living it. History should be about fighting.'

'Well, it will be after half term. You'll have to be patient. Meanwhile, you have to make an Anderson shelter.'

'What's that?'

'A bunker in the garden. People sat in them during air raids. You have to make one, then find out what it would be like to be inside with bombs falling all around.'

'But how can I?' I said.

Mum sighed. That was a good question. We'd normally go to the library because there was much more there than what we could find online. We'd look at books and old newspapers. We'd done that before; but now the libraries were all shut. Mum said we'd have to make do with the internet, but then her eyes lit up.

'I know what we can do!' she exclaimed.

'What?' I asked – but Mum wouldn't tell me. This is because she'd glanced up at the wall clock. It was nearly eight o'clock. Her eyes popped open and she stood up from her chair.

'We're going to miss Bobby Bunns!' she cried. She ran upstairs and got changed, after which we had to stand in the living room in front of the TV – while I groaned. I really wanted to know about her plan. I asked her again what it was but she just started shaking her arms out, as Bobby Bunns came onto the screen. First, he did his big cheesy smile, which is so wrong for that time of day. How could he be so cheerful IN THE MORNING? I would have really liked to ask him that, but I couldn't, of course, so I just sighed as he started doing these stretches, his body so muscly he looked like those balloons at parties that you turn into sausage dogs.

'Come on, Cym,' Mum said. Mum was bending over, her bum sticking out like she was learning to skateboard. 'Get into it!'

'Why?' I groaned.

'Because it's good for us. It's a great way to start the day.'

'It's not. You know what is?'

'What?'

'Pancakes.'

'Nonsense. We've got to keep fit.'

'Okay. But why can't keeping fit involve a football? Why do we have to do it with this bloke? He's grinning like someone who's got frozen on Zoom.'

Mum didn't answer. Her eyes were glued to the screen.

'Mum?'

'What? Oh. Er . . . because he's an expert.'

'Is he? He's not dressed like one. Why hasn't he got a shirt on?'

'Who cares? Sorry, I mean, who knows? He probably gets hot under those TV lights.'

She was right there. Bobby Bunns was doing star jumps now. 'Eeugh,' I said. 'He's getting all sweaty.'

'He is,' Mum said. 'Isn't he?'

'Mum, you've stopped.'

'Have I? Right, yes. Come on, Cym!'

And I had no choice but to do star jumps and burpees and press-ups and sit-ups, until Bobby Bunns

goodbye.

'See you tomorrow!' he said.

'Yes,' Mum replied, gazing at the screen again like it was some incredible work of art. 'We will DEFINITELY see you tomorrow.'

Then she just stood, with her hands on her hips, panting, until Bobby Bunns was replaced by the news.

And only THEN did Mum tell me her plan.

CHAPTER TEN

'We're going to see Mrs Stebbings.'

'Really?' I said. 'Honestly?'

'Yes,' Mum said. 'I mean, if we're safe. If you keep a good distance. Otherwise . . .'

'I will,' I insisted, thinking Mum might be feeling a bit guilty about my shirt, which is why she was allowing this. I'd make sure she was safe, though. 'I'll stay wherever you want. PROMISE.'

Mum nodded, which was great news – and not just because of finding out about the Home Front. As I said before, Mrs Stebbings holds the EXTREMELY IMPORTANT position of Chief Dinner Lady at our school. She's also one of my favourite people, EVER. This is due, in large part, to something that should, in my opinion, be officially classed as one of the Wonders of the World.

Mrs Stebbings's World-famous . . . *drum-roll, drum-roll* . . .

STICKY TOFFEE PUDDING

The first time you taste Mrs Stebbings's World-famous Sticky Toffee Pudding, it is recommended that you stand very close to something very soft. This is in case you faint. The experience, you see, is like a thousand very small angels climbing into your mouth and setting off a million golden explosions on your tongue. Mrs Stebbings's sticky toffee pudding is, I believe, the Jackie Chapman of sticky toffee puddings, and if there was a Sticky Toffee Pudding Athletic, Mrs Stebbings's sticky toffee pudding would certainly be the captain. This is because of its smell, and its flavour, but mostly because it is the stickiest sticky toffee pudding that can, and has, ever been made. Lance once got told off because Mr Ashe asked him a maths question and all he could say, was 'Tfwo Hufnphred anf firffy-fwee'. And that was nearly an hour after lunchtime!

But don't get me wrong. I don't just love Mrs Stebbings for her sticky toffee pudding. That would be terrible. I also love her for her delicious lemon surprise and her jam roly-poly. And it's not just food. As I mentioned, Mrs Stebbings is a MASSIVE Charlton fan! On Mondays, Lance and I go and find her at breaktime to discuss the previous game. On Fridays we discuss the one that's coming up. Her face when I brought my shirt in really was a picture: it was like Mabel's would be if she actually saw a REAL unicorn. So, as a fellow Charlton fan, Mrs Stebbings would be bound to help me with my project, and she would understand how terrible it was that I'd lost my shirt. She'd understand, from really feeling it.

'Can we go and see her now?' I said.

Well, I knew what Mum would normally have said to that: we'd *BORING BORING* been out *BORING BORING* once today *BORING BORING* already. Mrs Stebbings only lives round the corner, though, and our earlier trip hadn't exactly gone to plan. So Mum gave in, and ten minutes later she was peering out of the door. A man was going by so she ducked back in and I looked at her.

'And she'll know about this Home Front thing?'

Mum nodded.

'And she'll be up?'

'It's late enough,' Mum said. 'She's normally in school before now, getting your amazing lunches started.'

'Great,' I said, and we headed out.

The street was empty. Mrs Stebbings lives halfway

towards my school so we went in that direction, hurrying to the corner, then turning up towards the nursery I used to go. Maybe it was finding that Thomas beaker, but I had flashes of being there: or of someone who used to be me. It was like he was a different person. That was weird and it was also weird when we got up to the main road. Normally, it's busy. There are builders from the new development, people going to work, plus all the other parents taking their kids to school. It was almost empty, though, and the people who *were* around stood out. Did that person have coronavirus? Or that one? Were they likely to give it to us?

I shook those thoughts away, though. We waited at the pelican crossing and I blinked, imagining actually going on past Mrs Stebbings's house like I normally did – to school. Lance would be waiting at the top of the steps. He'd ask if I'd seen highlights of the Charlton game (answer: yes). Veronique would be in the playground. She'd ask if I'd seen some documentary on molecules, or plankton. Or the molecules in plankton (answer: no). I'd play football with Billy and Lance, and Vi and Daisy, who were both in the Lewisham girls' team. Maybe the new girl would want to join in. I frowned because it all seemed great. So . . .

SHOCK HORROR!

. . . did I actually MISS school?

Was Veronique having a dangerous influence on me?

No. It wasn't school I missed. What I missed were the people, one of whom was Mrs Stebbings, who sort of *is* St Saviour's. Every year, the Year Sixes all vanish off to new schools. New Reception kids arrive. The teachers come and go too sometimes, but not Mrs Stebbings. She's eighty-three years old and has actually been at our school longer than my Mum's been alive!

'They'd have to drag me out,' she said once, when Mum asked her about retiring. 'Wouldn't leave here if Jackie Chapman himself got down on one knee.'

'Wouldn't you marry him, then?'

'Course I would, Cymbeline, though I'd have to bump off my Albert first, wouldn't I? But it'd be one week in Margate with Captain Jack rubbing sun cream on my shoulders, then back to St Saviour's to feed you lot.'

Mum laughed and I did, too – because there was no WAY Mrs Stebbings would bump off Albert. They've been married for ever. Mum told me that they actually first met when they were little. They lived on the same street. Now, they were inseparable. Mr Stebbings is retired but every morning he puts on a suit and tie and walks Mrs Stebbings to school. And he picks her up afterwards. On Saturdays they have lunch in Blackheath and they stop on the way to see our football matches in the Lewisham League.

'GO ON, CYMBELINE!' Mr Stebbings hollers, whenever I get the ball. When the ref gets something wrong, Mrs Stebbings goes bananas.

'You should have gone to Specsavers!' she bellows.

In our last game before lockdown, the ref actually told her off and she went even redder than her Charlton scarf. No one minds, though, not even the opposition, because everyone knows Mrs Stebbings. And they all know that she's a legend. I was glad we were going to see her. It would be like a little taste of school (without the maths).

And that gave me an idea.

'Mum,' I said, as we turned up Morpeth Hill. 'You know the STP?'

'What?' Mum looked at me.

'Sticky toffee pudding! That Mrs Stebbings makes?'

'Of course. You talk about it in your sleep.'

'That is NOT true.'

'Maybe not, but you would swap me for a bowlful, wouldn't you?'

'That IS true.'

'Thanks. But what of it?'

'Well, Mrs Stebbings isn't cooking it at school now, is she?'

'No. So?'

'It occurred to me.'

Mum looked wary. 'What did?'

'Something potentially terrible. What if Mrs Stebbings gets out of practice?'

'Making the STP?'

'Yes. What if she forgets how to make it so brilliantly?'

'A whole school full of children would be devastated.'

'Exactly! So I was thinking. To keep Mrs Stebbings IN practice – for everyone's benefit – why don't we make her an offer?'

'What kind of offer?'

'To make US some! Once a week. She could make

it and we could pick it up from her front garden. We could taste it and give her a quality report. You know, just to make sure that it's . . .'

'Oh,' Mum said, her hand tightening in mine as she came to sudden stop.

I stopped too, of course – and looked down. I thought there must be something on the pavement. I thought Mum didn't want me to step in it, if you know what I mean – but it wasn't that. And it wasn't someone about to walk too close to us, either.

Mum was staring up the road.

And, when I followed her gaze, I saw what she was staring at.

An ambulance.

Its blue lights were flashing silently.

And Mum was staring at the frail old lady who was slowly being led towards it.

CHAPTER ELEVEN

It took me a few seconds to realise.

Who it was.

This was because we were still quite a way from Mrs Stebbings's house – and because I'd NEVER seen her like this. At school, she's always in her dinner-lady uniform. Now she was in a dressing gown. At school, she swings metal dishes about and hoists up the trays with the dirty plates in. She barrels down the middle of the hall, booming at us all: 'Get it down you!' But, now, two ambulance people in masks and gloves were holding her arms. And she definitely wasn't barrelling. She was shuffling, each step a real effort as she tried to catch her breath. When she came to the ramp at the back of the ambulance, she stared at it like it was a mountain. She stopped, took a deeper breath, and then nodded, and the ambulance people led her up it.

And she was inside.

I didn't know what to do. Neither did Mum. All we could do was stare, as one of the ambulance people came back out and hurried round to the front. She climbed into the cab and the ambulance reversed, its tyres crunching on some loose stones on the road. Then, almost before I knew what was happening, the ambulance went past us towards the main road.

'Mum?' I said.

But Mum didn't answer. Instead, she looked both ways and then walked me across the road.

Mr and Mrs Stebbings live about halfway up Morpeth Hill, on the corner of a little cul-de-sac. Their house has a small front garden with a greenhouse. When we walk to school, Mr Stebbings is often inside it, but he wasn't today. The greenhouse was empty and the house looked empty, too. Mum still went through the gate, though. She bunched her sleeve over her fingers and rang the doorbell. She stepped back and waited but when nothing happened, she bent down to the letter box.

'Albert?' she called. 'Are you there?'

There was no reply, so Mum straightened and stepped across the Stebbings's little front lawn. She put her hand on her forehead and peered through the living-room window. Then she reached into her bag and pulled her phone out.

'Who are you calling?' I asked, as she tapped in her passcode. She told me she was calling school, which was still open for the children of key workers. I was about to ask why, when Mum stood up a little straighter.

'Oh, hello, Linda,' she said. Linda is Daisy's mum, but she also works in the school office. Mum told her about Mrs Stebbings, then bit her lip as she listened. 'And Albert's not here,' Mum went on. 'Have you heard anything?'

Linda clearly hadn't because the next thing Mum did was sigh. She told Linda that she'd call her back. She hung up and then looked around, as if Mr Stebbings might suddenly appear. He didn't; we could only see a squirrel, on top of the garden fence. I peered up and down the hill, before turning back to Mum.

'Their car's gone,' I said.

The Stebbings have this classic old car called a Morris Minor. It's Mr Stebbings's pride and joy, and it's really distinctive – bright red, of course. It wasn't there.

'Do you think he went on ahead of the ambulance? To the hospital?'

Mum shook her head. 'He'd have followed it. If he was going. And he wouldn't be allowed in anyway. So . . .'

'Yes?'

'I don't know. Maybe he went out.'

'To the shops?'

'Maybe. Do you know which supermarket they go to, Cym?'

I sighed – and said I didn't. The nearest shop is the Tesco on the outskirts of Lewisham, though. So, after Mum had left a note for Mr Stebbings, we walked down there. Again, it was weird, though not because there was no one about this time. It was the opposite: the Tesco was really busy. There was a long queue of people who were just waiting to get in. The car park was full too, with cars circling for spaces like sharks.

But there was no Morris Minor.

Mum sighed again, while I asked what we should do. Mum thought for a second and then shook her head.

'We'd better go home.'

'But that means that Mr Stebbings will go back to an empty house. He'll really worry.'

'I know, but he'll see my note. He'll call me. Okay?'

I nodded reluctantly, but I wasn't happy. We set off towards home, though you don't have to go along the main road from there. We went the back way, past the new flats, Mum holding my hand a bit tighter than she normally would. She didn't say anything but I knew what she was thinking – because I was thinking it too.

This virus thing: up until now it had been something general. It was something on the news: the daily figures about how many people had got it and how many were in hospital. It had affected us, of course, by stopping our school and making us miss our friends. It had never seemed that close to us, though. Now it did, and I shivered to think of Mrs Stebbings. Thinking of Mr Stebbings was just as bad. I didn't want him coming home to Mum's note. We were his friends, weren't we? We had to tell him in person.

And I realised how.

'Mum,' I said, stopping suddenly, like she had earlier. 'Look.'

We'd passed the flats. We'd walked past the hairdresser's and were just approaching the DLR station (and the bridge where I normally get Mum to be a troll). I didn't point at them, though.

I pointed to the allotments.

The allotments are a big piece of land, with a wall round the edge. It's owned by the council. The land is divided into strips, which people can rent. Our neighbours on the corner rent one and they give us stuff: potatoes and plums, and these flowers called sweet peas that Mum likes. Stephan says he'd love an allotment, but it's not just individuals who can have them.

Our school has got one, too.

We've had it for ever, apparently. It's paid for by the Parents' Forum, who run all the summer fayres and Christmas parties. A different year group goes down on the first Thursday of every month. We pick and plant things and collect frogspawn from the little pond.

There's also an Allotment Club after school – on

Mondays. I went a couple of times in Year Three, when we had Mrs Robinson. Football training was changed to the same day so I stopped going, though that wasn't the only reason. It was also the waiting! On my first week, we dug holes and put strawberry plants in. That was fine, but the following week, there were NO strawberries! In fact, NOTHING had happened. These were LAZY plants and no mistake, something I thought the other kids would be annoyed about too, especially Marcus Breen who is SUCH a scoffer. He was in hysterics, though, which I couldn't understand until I put a pair of the school wellies on.

And *felt* something.

Marcus cracked up even more. With the horrible feeling that he must have *done* something, I grabbed hold of my left welly's heel. I pulled it off and tipped it upside down. When nothing came out I stuck my hand in (hopping like I was on a pogo stick). I fished around and pulled out what I thought was a piece of Marcus's old chewing gum, which would have been disgusting enough. But it wasn't. With utter horror I stared at my fingers and saw something long and slimy and the most disgusting shade of brown.

I, Cymbeline Igloo, was holding a slug.

Did I laugh? Did I raise my eyes and shake my head? Did I say, 'Good one, Marcus, great joke, that'?

No.

I screamed. And I tried to throw the slug on the ground – but it was curling round my fingers. It didn't want to come off! I screamed again and, still on one leg, I lurched to the left – into a stack of plant pots, which went flying. And then I lurched to the right – into Mrs Robinson, who also went flying.

In fact, we both did.

Into the pond.

'Cym,' Mum said, next morning, when we were about to leave for school. 'Why is there a frog peeking out of your coat pocket?'

That was the last time I'd been to Allotment Club.

I did know this, though: Mr Stebbings loves gardening – and he helps. He goes down to the allotment at the weekends *and* he also gets all the tools ready for Allotment Club.

On Mondays.

Allotment Club wasn't on, of course, but the allotment would still need looking after, wouldn't it?

I pulled Mum's arm and led her across the road, not having to explain because I could tell that she understood – and because the allotment gates were open.

We walked through them, immediately looking round for Mr Stebbings. The St Saviour's allotment is near the entrance, the top of it dug with little trenches for seeds. Beyond these – a bit further down – were some low plants that I didn't recognise, then came herb bushes, one of which we've got in our garden, too. After those were rows of runner beans and more low plants, before there was a really bushy bit at the bottom. These plants were tall – taller even than me – with bamboo poles to hold them up.

And they were moving.

Not very much. More than the wind would have made them move, though. Mum and I looked at each other. I was about to call out but Mum squeezed my arm; she didn't want me to startle Mr Stebbings. Instead, we walked down on the outside of the row, until we'd passed the runner beans. Mum stopped.

'Albert?'

Mum's voice was quiet. Nervous-sounding. I knew why. We were going to have to do something awful: tell Mr Stebbings about Mrs Stebbings. When there was no reply, Mum sighed and we moved on a bit.

'Albert?' she said again, though louder this time. Mr Stebbings must have heard because the tops of the bushes stopped moving and I expected him to appear. I braced myself for that, though when he didn't, I was confused. Mum was, too, her face wrinkling up as she edged a little closer.

Which is when it happened.

Flash!

A shape SHOT out from behind the big plants. It moved so fast that I couldn't take it in, especially as it disappeared behind another row of plants on the next allotment. The surprise had also made Mum stumble, and I had to turn away from the shape as I helped her stay upright. But, when I did turn back, I saw it again – sprinting into the open.

And I gasped.

And I STARED.

Not at Mr Stebbings.

No.

I stared at the kid with the baseball cap – though it wasn't on his head his time. It was in his hand, and he managed to drop it as he leaped towards an old dustbin which was propped up against the far wall. The kid jumped at the bin and launched himself up to the top of the wall. He hooked one leg over as the word jumped from my chest.

'STOP!'

And the kid did stop. He turned and stared at me from the top of the wall. The first thing I did was gasp, because I'd got it wrong. This wasn't a boy! I was looking at a tall, skinny girl, with straight black hair falling down over her face. She looked back at me and, for a split second, our eyes met. Then she turned round again and flung her other leg over the top of the wall – as I glared.

At her shirt.

HER shirt?

No!

MY SHIRT!

CHAPTER TWELVE

I sprinted towards the bin. I jumped up at it, sending it flying backwards as I grabbed the top of the wall. I'm not tall, though. Unlike the girl, who had now vanished, I couldn't hitch my legs up. After four attempts I just dangled there, with a VERY empty feeling below me.

'Help!' I screamed.

Mum grabbed the bottom of my legs and I let go. We both tumbled backwards, and when I looked up, a shape was standing over us.

'Cymbeline?' Mr Stebbings said.

Mum and I scrambled to our feet as Mr Stebbings walked over to the baseball cap. Bending slowly, he picked it up, and showed us what was in it: raspberries.

'Third time in two weeks,' he said. He scratched the top of his head, which was fully covered by thick, white hair. 'Well done for nearly catching the cheeky blighter. Strange thing is, they're not ripe. But anyway, don't normally see you down here, young man, 'specially not after the slug incident. What's going on, then?'

'Albert,' Mum began.

There was silence for a second. But then Mum told him. She explained that we'd wanted to talk to him and Mrs Stebbings about my project. She described going up Morpeth Hill – and seeing the ambulance. Mum explained that we hadn't even had time to speak to Mrs Stebbings. Mr Stebbings looked winded.

'I knew she wasn't right,' he said.

Mum sighed. 'When, Albert?'

'Last night.' Mr Stebbings closed his eyes for a second and I looked at his gnarled face, the lines on it like the knots in an old tree. 'She said she was feeling off. I sent her to bed. She called me an old fusspot. I got up this morning and she was sleeping, so I thought I'd leave her. I didn't want to wake her. Poor love, must have called the ambulance herself. Where did they take her to? Which hospital?'

'Lewisham,' Mum said. 'At least, they turned in that direction. But it has to be that one, doesn't it? We'll . . . come with you.'

'What?' Mr Stebbings said. He looked horrified and he took a step back from us.

'You've got your car down here, haven't you?'

'Yes. Parked round the back.'

'Then we'll come.'

'No.' Mr Stebbings stepped back even further. 'You should stay clear of me. Probably got it too, haven't I? Thanks for coming to tell me. That was very good of you, but I'll . . . I'll just go on my own.'

And there was nothing we could do to persuade him. Mum did try, something that made me really proud of her, given how nervous she was about the virus. But all we could do was watch as Mr Stebbings put a wheelbarrow away and then locked the St Saviour's shed up. We followed him to his car and watched as he got in. The Morris Minor pulled away and Mum and I waved, though not like we normally would. Not with any force. We just held our hands up, before Mum put one of hers round my shoulders. I looked up at her.

'She will be all right?' I said. 'Won't she?'

And I expected Mum to say 'Yes, of course'. I really wanted her to say that. But Mum was silent until the Morris Minor had turned up past the hairdresser's and was out of sight.

'Mum?'

'Come on, Cym,' she said.

CHAPTER THIRTEEN

At home, the house seemed echoey. Empty. I don't know why. Perhaps it was because Mum sent me into the kitchen while she went into the living room to call school again. It was obviously to give them an update on Mrs Stebbings and I thought of her – or tried to.

She was in the hospital, and I know Lewisham Hospital. I've been there loads of times, and the staff there are brilliant. But, without going there in person to see Mrs Stebbings, I couldn't picture her. All I could see was how she'd looked going into the ambulance. I saw her taking wheezy breaths as they led her up the ramp. I kept seeing that until Mum came through to the kitchen and took the baseball cap off me, emptying the raspberries into a bowl. We looked at each other for a long second and, once again, I wanted her to tell me that Mrs Stebbings would be okay, that she'd be out in a day or so and 'right as rain'. Instead, she just gave me a hug, before putting her hands up on her hips in a way that told me she'd decided: we had to just get on with things now.

'Right then,' she said.

What that meant, was school. Going from still and sombre to brisk and quick, Mum got the laptop from the kitchen and plugged it into the printer. She printed off that week's timetable and took it, and the laptop, back to the kitchen table. I followed, finding it odd that so much had happened that day already. I was glad that I had something else to focus on, though. To get on with. I didn't even moan when I saw what the first thing was: English comprehension. It's not that I don't like books. I love books! It's having to UNDERSTAND books that I don't like. It sort of sucks all the flavour out of them. I was prepared to do it, though – but I was spared.

'Oh!' Mum exclaimed. She was peering at the laptop now, obviously looking at her email from Mr Ashe.

'What?'

Mum didn't answer. Instead, she ran out of the kitchen and thumped up the stairs. She came back with a school jumper, which she pushed down over my head. I was confused for a second – but it had to mean that we had our first live video call, which we'd been promised. I was actually going to see my teacher! And some of my classmates! I was so excited, until Mum pulled out what I can only describe as an INSTRUMENT OF PARENTAL TORTURE (though you might know it by the name 'hairbrush'). We did have to wear uniform but there were no instructions at all about having neat hair, something I tried to explain. Mum didn't listen; she attacked me with the thing until Mr Ashe's face popped up on the screen in front of me.

'Hello, Cymbeline!' he said.

After batting Mum's hands away, I said hello back. I then watched as the screen changed, reminding me of a time-lapse thing we'd watched once, of flowers suddenly blooming. One by one, more faces blinked up on the screen. I assumed they were my friends, but were they? Had I joined the wrong class? When the first face came up, I squinted at it, unable to recognise who it was until I realised: Billy! I thought he was wearing a wig but he wasn't. It was his hair – it was really long. I laughed again when Danny Jones popped up – because he was worse. His hair's really frizzy at the best of times, but now he looked like he should have been marching up and down outside Buckingham Palace. The next face wasn't such a surprise – Daisy's got long hair anyway – but she made me laugh too, because I could see food on her chin, like normal! Every morning at school, Vi and I played a game called 'Guess What Daisy Had For Breakfast'. When Vi popped up next I was about to shout 'Jam on toast!' but I could tell she wasn't paying attention. She was hissing at her mum to get out of sight, though her mum was madly trying to remove a clothes horse from behind Vi, which was covered in pants and bras.

'Morning, Mrs Delap!' said Mr Ashe.

Vi put her hands over her eyes and then another face appeared: Lance. Marcus Breen was next, though he didn't know that his camera was on. He was looking to the left, his finger jammed so far up his nose that I thought it might come out of one of his ears. When his mum shouted, 'Marcus, you're on!' he jerked upright, pulled the finger out, then turned on his microphone with THE SAME FINGER!

Talk about the need for hand sanitiser.

It was strangely good to see Marcus, though. In fact, and in spite of what had happened that morning, it was good to see everyone. I'd done Zooms with Lance, and with Veronique, but this was different. It was especially good to see Mr Ashe in the middle of us all: right there, like he usually is.

'Hello, Blue Group,' he said, in his big, cheerful voice.

We all said 'Hello' back, and I got ready for whatever we'd be talking about. But another face appeared. This time I thought that someone else *had* got the wrong link, but it was the new girl, Semira. She'd only been at school for a few real days before lockdown began. It didn't feel like she was one of us yet, and Veronique was right: that must have been weird for her. It was probably even weirder now, doing a video call with people she hardly knew, and a teacher she'd only met a couple of times.

Mr Ashe made her welcome, though. Once she seemed settled, he asked us all to keep our cameras on – and pay attention. I thought that meant we'd start the English comprehension and I took a breath.

But I was wrong.

'We're not doing a lesson,' Mr Ashe explained. 'I just want to find out how you're getting on.'

Excellent! Everyone started gabbling until Mr Ashe held his palms up.

'One at a time!' he said. 'How about you, Veronique? How've you been finding things?'

I shifted in my chair, and sighed to myself. I already knew how Veronique was getting on, though it was still a shock when she went on about how much work she'd done. It made me feel guilty and it was a relief when Mr Ashe turned to Billy, who just said he was bored. Danny Jones agreed, while Daisy groaned.

'It's my dad,' she explained.

Mr Ashe frowned. 'What's wrong with him?'

Daisy leaned in to the camera. 'He's at home! Normally, he goes out. He wears a suit and disappears, but now he's always trying to talk to me about stuff. And he won't shave. He looks like a bad Father Christmas, and he plays this music. It's called heavy metal, apparently, and it was popular when he was our age. But it's terrible. It sounds like tigers being murdered.'

Mr Ashe winced. He said there was NO excuse for heavy metal at all.

'I'll put that in the next email to parents,' he said. 'And suggest some Stevie Wonder. How about you, Vi?' he added.

Vi turned her mic on then – and sounded just as annoyed as Daisy. I thought she'd just moan about not being able to play football, but she had a different problem. 'If,' she hissed, 'I have to spend one more day locked up with my older brother, I am going to explode!'

'Franklin?' Mr Ashe said. 'I taught him. He's a delightful boy!'

Vi looked stunned. 'Maybe he WAS. Now he's at secondary school he thinks he's God. I'm still at "baby school", apparently. And Mum's given him the best laptop, of course! My one's ancient. She must have bought it off an archaeologist.'

We all laughed at that, and I imagined some scientists digging up Vi's laptop. But I didn't laugh for long. It was Semira's turn and – in a quiet voice – she told us that she didn't have a laptop.

'I just use my Mum's phone,' she explained.

'That's not ideal,' Mr Ashe said.

'No. And my brothers need it too, so we have to take turns. Outside school it's hard too. We have no garden. We're not near a park so there's nowhere really to go.'

I thought about how close Mulberry Park was and felt guilty again, while Mr Ashe sympathised. He told Semira that he'd try to get her a laptop from school, and that he'd think of places for her to go, seeing as she was new to the area. Then he sat up.

'Cymbeline?' he said.

Even though it was onscreen, I could feel everyone looking at me – just like we were in class. I should have been pleased – because I'd done the Super Seven. Stephan was wrong, though. Without any proof, it would sound stupid, and I couldn't complain about losing my Charlton shirt either, not after what Semira had told us about what she was dealing with. I just sighed, and linked my fingers together.

'Does everyone know about Mrs Stebbings?' I asked.

No one on the screen answered. A few people frowned, though not Mr Ashe. Calmly, he said he did know. He said that he was just about to talk to us about it. And he did. I thought he'd be all soft. Reassuring, like how I'd wanted Mum to be. But he said that Mrs Stebbings was very unwell. He said she was in hospital and that we all had to think about her. Everyone on the screen went still. We all had our mics off, but I could tell that no one was speaking. Veronique lowered her head a bit. Billy started to blink, while Daisy swallowed and looked a bit scared. Vi just looked determined.

'Can we go and see her?' she asked.

Mr Ashe sighed. He explained that visitors weren't being allowed into hospitals. Daisy asked if that meant that even Mr Stebbings wasn't allowed and, again, Mr Ashe said no.

'So she's all alone?' Lance asked.

Mr Ashe said yes, and it wasn't ideal – but we had to be positive. Again, he told us to hold Mrs Stebbings in our thoughts, but I frowned. We just had to *think* about her? Was that all, considering everything that SHE did for US?

No!

It couldn't be.

And it wasn't.

Because, right then, staring at my classmates on the screen, I, Cymbeline Igloo, had a **BRILLIANT** idea.

CHAPTER FOURTEEN

'We're all doing history projects, right?'

I waited a second until Mr Ashe nodded.

'Well,' I went on, 'Mum and I were watching the news. There was this report about people in hospital. They couldn't be visited but if they could hear people's voices, it made a big difference to them.'

'Right,' Mr Ashe said. 'And you think we could do something like that?'

'Well, why don't we do our World War Two projects for Mrs Stebbings? She grew up around that time, didn't she? She was only young then but she was actually part of the Home Front. My mum told me. We could do the things that she'd be really interested in, to remind her. We could make a video, you know, of everyone's contributions. Then we could show it to her!'

Mr Ashe sat up. 'That's a great idea!' he said. 'But you'd all need to work on different things to make it really good.'

'I'll do Charlton!' Lance bellowed.

'What?' Mr Ashe said. 'In the war?'

'Yeah! Some of our players joined up, you know? There's a memorial outside the stadium. They had this special War Cup and we won it. My grandad told me. He said there were bomb-spotters at the games, who had to look out for planes coming over. Imagine that!'

'Did they hit the pitch?'

'No, but some were close. My grandad said that a massive bomb hit Charlton station.'

'That's a great idea, Lance.' Mr Ashe was nodding.

'Thanks. I'll find out who the players were, and what they said about it.'

Mr Ashe said that was fantastic. Mrs Stebbings would LOVE that. I agreed and so did everyone else. No one was still now. Everyone was really animated. I was about to say that I'd join in with Lance, but Billy and Marcus put their hands up before me. Mr

Ashe said three was enough and asked what else we could do.

Vi put her hand up and I thought she'd want to do football, too – but she's an even bigger fan of the STP than me. Whenever we've had it during the past year she's taken a tiny bit home, for Franklin. Not to give him. No. She eats it in front of him to wind him up.

'Who's at a rubbish school now?' she asks him.

Also, last year, she spent ages doing a painting of the STP, not telling anyone why until we saw where she'd stuck it up: on our 'Religions of the World' display.

So, Vi was going to do Food in World War Two. Daisy said she'd help. Semira asked if she could do a wartime map, which Mr Ashe said was a fabulous idea.

Veronique said she'd do music. 'I'll learn something for the piano.'

'Perfect,' Mr Ashe said. 'We'll Meet Again.'

'In another video call?'

'No! It's a famous wartime song, sung by Vera Lynn. Can you find it?'

Veronique said she would – and asked me to help.

I'm no good at music, though. The only instrument I've ever tried to learn is the recorder, in Year Two. I took one home to practise and played it every day until I lost it. I couldn't find it for weeks, until I spotted it under Mum's bed.

'I wonder how it got there,' Veronique said.

So, I wasn't going to do music. Or football or food. And that left a problem. It had been my idea, and I was proud of it. But what could I do?

'A drawing?' Mr Ashe suggested. 'That's your thing, isn't it? As well as football, of course.'

I nodded because Mr Ashe was right. Art is the one thing at school I am good at, something I must have got from my mum. It was a good idea – but I wanted to do something specific for Mrs Stebbings. 'A drawing of what?' I said.

'Your Anderson shelter?'

'But I haven't made one yet. It'll take ages.'

'Then how about her street?' Veronique suggested.

'What?'

'Where Mrs Stebbings grew up.'

'Where she met Mr Stebbings?'

'Yes.'

'But how can I?'

'Easy! It's really near you. She told me once. It's close to our allotments. You could draw her street, and maybe put her in it as a little girl. How about that, Cymbeline?'

How about it? I nodded. Yes. I would draw the exact street that Mrs Stebbings grew up on, with the street sign and everything. Though I had a problem.

'What's it called? The street, I mean?'

But no one knew. I could easily find out, though.

The call ended, people freezing in different, weird positions before disappearing completely. I waved goodbye and then asked Mum to phone Mr Stebbings.

'Though don't tell him why you want to know. I want it to be a surprise,' I insisted.

'Okay,' Mum said, shutting the laptop. 'But later. We need to give him some space at the moment.'

'All right, but if he does tell you the street name, can we go there today?'

'Uh-uh. That would make three times out. Not happening. Get on with your school work and we'll think about it tomorrow, okay?'

It was frustrating, but I had to agree.

Mum asked if I needed her for an hour. She wanted to go upstairs to work on her sketch of the river. I said fine.

'But come and get me if there's anything you need to ask me about that English comprehension, yes?'

I nodded at that, but when I looked at the English comprehension I suddenly felt REALLY tired. How could I possibly concentrate on that when I'd been up so early? The answer was that I couldn't, though actually I didn't have to. I had another piece of homework to do, didn't I? I could do that first. I shut the laptop and went outside to the shed. I got a spade out and started digging up the lawn, really having a good go at it. By the time Mum came down again I'd made a big hole, which I was standing in.

'Cymbeline!' Mum gasped. 'WHAT ON EARTH ARE YOU DOING?!'

'Homework,' I explained.

'HOMEWORK?'

'Yes, and I could do with some help, actually.'

'Help?'

'Getting deep enough is going to be really hard.'

'Deep enough for what?!'

I frowned. 'An Anderson shelter! The bunker in the

garden, remember? We have to make one, though I don't see how Semira's going to manage.'

'*What?* Who's Semira?'

'The new girl. She hasn't got a garden. She lives in a flat. Now, what should we use for a roof?'

'OH, CYMBELINE!

Mum said.

Mum helped me shovel the soil back in, and then we trod the grass down on the top. She was really cross with me, which was TOTALLY unfair. If Mr Ashe had wanted us to make a MODEL Anderson shelter, he should have said so! Teachers, some advice: good communication is EVERYTHING.

Mum STILL blamed me, though, and her mood wasn't helped by the news when we watched it again later. Apparently, the government hadn't got enough protective equipment for the doctors and nurses, or the people working in care homes. Worse, people were saying the government didn't lock us all down early enough, which was why so many people got the virus. Was this why Mrs Stebbings caught it? It made me really cross, and I was still cross in the morning.

Because Mum woke me up early AGAIN.

CHAPTER FIFTEEN

It wasn't to go the park, though (this time).

'What is it now?' I moaned.

'I managed to speak to Mr Stebbings,' Mum explained. I pushed myself up on to an elbow and looked into her eyes. There was a question that I both wanted to ask and didn't want to ask at the same time.

'How's Mrs Stebbings?' I said.

'Stable.'

I tried to take it in. 'What does that mean?'

'That she's the same as when we saw her.'

'Oh.'

'But we, however, have a problem.'

'Do we?'

'Yes.' Mum sighed. 'Food. Or the lack of. I just can't get a delivery.'

'From the supermarket?'

'Yes. All the slots are full.'

'So . . . we won't have anything to eat?'

'Not unless I go shopping.'

'Are you sure?' I sat up properly, and shoved the duvet off. 'Didn't you say that shops aren't very safe at the moment?'

Mum looked nervous. 'I did. But we need so many things. And I promised to go for Albert – Mr Stebbings. He has to self-isolate. So . . . ?'

'Yes?'

Mum took a deep breath. 'Will you be okay?'

'I suppose. Can we just be quick, though? Not spend ages in there?'

'No,' Mum said. 'What I mean is, okay here?'

'Here? With who?'

'No one. Will you be okay . . . on your own?'

'WHAT?!' I said. And I shot up against my head board. On my own? Mum had NEVER left me alone before! Seeing my shock, she tried to reassure me, but I didn't need that. I'd always longed to be left on my own. I'd hit the biscuit tin! I'd eat all the chocolate fingers. Then I'd raid Mum's Chocolate Stash. Then I'd raid her Secret Chocolate Stash (SO not secret), after which I'd watch TV, which is off limits on school mornings. It was a vision of almost perfect happiness – until I got downstairs.

Mum looked relieved when I said I'd be fine, but the relief didn't last. As she got the breakfast things out, she looked jittery. Her movements were all dart-like, and jagged. I thought about how nervous she was on the street sometimes – because of Covid-19 – and I pictured her at the supermarket. If the Tesco was anything to go by, it would be busy. Loud. It would be stressful for her. Clearing the house out seemed to have calmed her down over the last couple of days, but what if that calmness was only temporary? We couldn't have a second clear out. We'd have nothing left. What if Mum found the supermarket difficult – and she was on her own? There was something else, too. She normally talks to Stephan in the morning and I could see that she had, because her phone was propped up against the Weetabix again. She hadn't told me all their latest news, though, or shown me today's unicorn picture by Mabel. So, was everything okay? I was about to ask, but yet another thought rushed into my head.

'Where's the shopping list?' I asked.

Mum pointed to the counter and I picked up an old gas-bill envelope. On the back, Mum had written 'Rice'. Then there was 'Pasta'. After that Mum had written 'Tins of tomatoes' and 'Porridge oats', which made me wince because I HATE porridge. It's like eating warmed-up sick. The list didn't get any better, though: underneath that, Mum had written 'Vegetables', 'Soap', 'Shampoo' and 'Toilet Roll!!'. Where was the raspberry ripple? Or the Jaffa cakes? The chocolate fingers? There were only seven left! I tossed the list down and pushed my bowl forward in disgust.

'I'm coming too,' I said.

We left ten minutes later. I wanted Mum to drive but she told me to think about the environment, which she clearly cared about more than my poor feet.

'We won't be able to bring much back,' I argued.

'Oh yes, we will,' Mum replied, and she showed me something else that she'd found when she was clearing out under the stairs: my old pushchair (with a Thomas the Tank Engine board book hanging off the side).

'It's perfect,' she said, as she put it up in our hall.

Mum stuffed the bottom of the pushchair with old

plastic bags. Then we set off. We got out of the house easily because no one was coming, but then Mum turned the wrong way – or so I thought. But we weren't, apparently, going to our usual supermarket. We were going to a different one because it had wider aisles.

'But will it still have the same things?' I asked, thinking mostly of the chocolate fingers.

'Of course!'

'Right then,' I said.

It wasn't far. We walked down Egerton Drive towards the River Thames, as I considered my strategy. The things that weren't on Mum's list: should I just come out and ask for them? It seemed the easiest thing to do, but what if Mum didn't agree to them all? No, I couldn't take that chance. What I'd do is just sneak things into the trolley when she wasn't looking – simple enough, as she gets distracted at the supermarket, checking all the packets for the recycling sign. I did worry a bit about the checkout, but she always has these long chats with the person behind the till. They could scan a whole elephant through and she wouldn't notice until we were back at home, and then she'd only complain if the elephant was wrapped in plastic like the cucumbers are.

By the time we got to this new supermarket, it was still only eight o'clock. There was a long queue, though, which we joined the back of, Mum immediately reaching underneath the pushchair. It wasn't for bags though. She pulled out a mask. Then she pulled out a scarf, followed by gloves and even a hat, which she proceeded to wrap herself in until all I could make out were her eyes. Still, if it made her feel safe, it was all right by me.

The queue moved along and, soon, Mum was squirting pink stuff on the trolley handle – while I stared. This supermarket was WELL posh. Everything was really shiny. The aisles were wider and the ceiling was higher too, though that didn't make it better because I could see shelves. And if you think that's normal for a supermarket, you're wrong. You usually see the stuff ON the shelves. But there wasn't much. A big sign said 'Fresh Produce', but whole sections were empty. Once we were properly inside, Mum did manage to scoop up some loose potatoes from the first aisle, but that was about it. There was nothing else until we saw a woman unloading bags of apples from a big trolley.

Mum normally only takes loose apples (because

of the plastic). She got a couple of the bags, though, while I felt weird. Here was something else that made the virus far more real to me. I didn't like to think about there not being enough food in the shops. There was something else I wanted to think about even less, though.

Cauliflower.

Cauliflower is NOT food. It's worse even than porridge (kind of like warmed-up sick that has dried out, but then been cooked again). It was, however, the only vegetable that the shop actually had and the idea that Mum might get some was so horrifying that I grabbed her by the sleeve.

'Mum!' I shouted. 'Someone just said that the pasta's running out!'

It worked.

Mum HAD seen the cauliflower and WAS heading in that direction. Immediately, however, she did a very quick three-point turn with the trolley, making a shopworker jump aside like a bullfighter. She shoved the trolley back to the top of the aisle, and turned. The next aisle was busier, which wouldn't normally have been a problem. Mum would have plodded along behind the other people, but not this time. She overtook one trolley and then tried to overtake another, waiting behind it like Lewis Hamilton, until a trolley coming the other way had gone. Again she sprinted forward, me trying to keep up as she reached out to the shelves. She didn't care about the recycling sign now. She just bunged stuff in, until we got to some fridges. Here she managed to snaffle some bacon (YES!) but she also got humous . . .

BEIGE FOOD ALERT!

BEIGE FOOD ALERT!

. . . as well as gnocchi, which I've only ever had once and which made me think I was eating boiled eyeballs.

After that, though, we came to the freezers, where my heart soared. On a normal day we'd leave the freezers until last so the stuff didn't melt, but I wasn't having that. I was getting the raspberry ripple, and I was getting it **NOW.**

Except . . .

I STARED.

And I STARED.

And I STARED.

And I STARED.

And I STARED.

And I STARED.

And I STARED.

And I STARED.

And I STARED.

And I STARED.

And I STARED.

And I STARED.

And there was no Raspberry Ripple.

Worse – there was no ice cream AT ALL! The only thing in the WHOLE freezer was a box of 'Fishless Vegan Fish Fingers', though how did that work? If they were fish fingers, how could they be vegan? Mum didn't care. She actually picked them up, before turning round to the shelves across from us. These were empty, except for swirls and drag-lines of a fine, white dust. I didn't understand – until I saw the sign:

FLOUR

But there was no flour! I'd already had to endure a WHOLE WEEKEND without pancakes. Was I going to have to undergo another one? And what if it didn't end there? What if there was ANOTHER pancake drought after that?

My chest began to heave.

I felt a little dizzy.

I think I was starting to have a panic attack, until I realised that it was even worse than I thought. If there was no flour, people had obviously bought it to make pancakes, because what else is flour for? And, if they were buying the flour to make pancakes, they would also be buying chocolate spread.

WHICH

WE'D

RUN

OUT

OF.

I didn't wait for Mum.

I left her behind, running my eyes across the shelves. At the top of the aisle I turned – into the next one. Then the next – where I spotted marmalade! I didn't want it because marmalade is not something I understand. It's made of oranges, which taste sweet, but marmalade tastes horrible. Do they put something horrible in with the oranges to make it taste like that? If so, why? But one thing I knew about marmalade is that it normally lives near the jam. And jam is normally right next to the chocolate spread!

It wasn't today, though, because next to the marmalade there was no jam. And, next to the no-jam, there was NO CHOCOLATE SPREAD. This realisation was like getting a rounders bat in the stomach, though it wasn't in fact the most terrible thing. Yes, I love chocolate spread. You can, however, use other things on pancakes. Mum has orange juice and sugar and it's pretty good. There is one food stuff, however, that has NO SUBSTITUTE. Thinking about it made me turn and run back to where Mum had been, though she was gone. I stared at the empty flour shelf and then moved along a bit, where I saw . . .

Soy Sauce.

And . . .

Worcestershire Sauce.

And . . .

Brown Sauce.

And . . .

Nothing.

Just a space, which rang like a cathedral bell inside my brain, hammering out the simple but undeniable truth.

There was no tomato ketchup.

CHAPTER SIXTEEN

My mouth went dry. My arms felt cold. Fish fingers flashed into my head and then vegan fishless fish fingers took their place. Was I really going to have to eat them, when they were naked? And what about other things?

Burgers?

It wasn't possible.

Sausages?!

NO! It would be a crime against my tastebuds. I shook my head and stared at the shelf, where the ketchup SHOULD HAVE BEEN, each bottle like a Charlton player lining up before kick-off. The gap seemed like the biggest, most cavernous space that I'd ever seen in my life – and I wasn't the only one to think that.

There was someone next to me. I turned, and saw a teenager. The teenager was about sixteen, a boy, possibly, though I wasn't totally sure. Like lots of teenagers, they were wearing a baggy hoodie and all I could see were strands of slimy hair hanging down beside a small amount of pale, gloomy face. But I didn't care because – as hard as you might find this to believe – the teenager and I bonded. They, too, were gawping at the empty shelf, which meant that they, too, were staring into a void of never-ending greyness. Their mouth dropped open and their hands went up to the sides of their face like that painting – The Scream. Then they turned – and our eyes met. I'll always remember that moment: two human beings, here on Planet Earth, joined in mutual torment at the idea of a life lived without tomato ketchup.

But the moment didn't last.

After a second or two, my gaze was – for some reason – drawn across the aisle. A man was standing there, inspecting some tins, a trolley full of nappies beside him. The shelves beyond him weren't full, though they did have some things on them: cereal packets. But they weren't what I was looking at.

I was looking at a MIRACLE.

How had it got there? I will never know. Perhaps it had just been unpacked in the wrong place. Perhaps someone had tried to hide it, meaning to come back later, but they'd forgotten. Whatever the reason, there, on the very top shelf across the aisle, above the cereal packets, was something red and glossy, its bright white lid shining like a star.

A bottle of tomato ketchup!

But I was stupid! My face must have registered my delight – because the teenager turned. Following my gaze, they also saw the bottle, and I'll give the teenager this: they were FAST. Breaking our bond, they darted across the aisle. If the tomato ketchup had been on a lower shelf I'd have been toast (with no chocolate spread on). But I was lucky. The teenager was bigger than me but not actually that tall. After three goes at leaping up it was clear: they couldn't reach the top shelf! SO relieved, I turned, about to run for Mum. But the teenager turned too – towards the man!

'DAD!' the teenager screamed. 'DAD! DAD! DAD! DAD!

DAD!'

And the man turned! He was clearly shocked, which might have been because he was actually being spoken to, which, apparently, is very rare with teenagers. The teenager started to pull the man along the aisle – towards the tomato ketchup! But I'd seen it first! That bottle was mine! In desperation I spun round, praying that Mum had followed me. But Mum was nowhere, so I took a huge gulp of air.

'Toilet roll!' I bellowed.

‘THEY’VE GOT TOILET ROLL ON AISLE SEVEN!!!’

The man's eyes jumped like table-tennis balls. Abandoning his trolley, he began to run. The teenager ran after him, yelling at him about the tomato ketchup, but the man didn't even pause. He pelted round the corner as I said, 'YES!' and gave myself a high five. But I didn't have much time. The man would very soon discover the absence of toilet roll on Aisle Seven, and listen to his teenager.

There was only one thing for it.

I put my right foot on the bottom shelf and thought about the last birthday party I'd been to before lockdown. It was Daisy's – at the climbing centre in Woolwich. True, I'd spent most of the time dangling in midair with a MASSIVE wedgie, but I did remember some of it. With my right foot secure, I put my left foot on the next shelf up (full of Cornflakes). I then put my right foot on the one above that (Shreddies) and then my right hand onto the one above that one (Sugar Puffs).

Creeeeeeak, went the shelves.

After that it was muesli. After that it was Weetabix. The tomato ketchup was only two more shelves up, though I couldn't go any higher. I'd have nothing to hold on to. I knew I had to reach out and so, gripping the edge of the muesli shelf, I did so, trying to keep my body flat against the shelves like the climbing instructor had said. Then I had to switch feet to keep my balance – which was scary. But I did it, and I was close. Then closer! The tomato ketchup was less than a metre away and I stretched out a hand.

And grabbed it.

Yes!

But I had a problem.

I'd only thought about climbing up. I hadn't thought about climbing down, and climbing down things is SO much harder. Furthermore, the shelves were not a wall at the climbing centre. They were beginning to feel . . . wobbly. Really wobbly. I had an image of the whole lot coming down and me landing in a pile of Cornflake boxes. Also, in the next aisle, I could make out the man and the teenager. The man was listening now. They were starting to come back! I put a shaky foot out towards the shelf below, but there was no way I could trust my weight to it.

So I jumped.

I did!

I stepped off the shelf, jumped into the air, and . . .

W!H!A!P!

I landed in the trolley full of nappies.

CHAPTER SEVENTEEN

It wasn't easy getting out of the shopping trolley. I was WELL jammed in (even though there was no jam). I managed though. Gripping the tomato ketchup I jumped onto the floor – and stared. The man and the teenager were just coming round the bottom of the aisle so I crouched down and hid behind a shopworker, who was staring up at the top of the shelves and frowning.

Then I legged it.

Mum was queuing at the checkouts. There were three trolleys in front of her, so I had time to go and get biscuits. I was forced to get random ones because there WERE no chocolate fingers. I suspected, and still suspect, that the teenager had bagged them all. I actually saw them near the pet food – looking left and right – and had to nip behind the coffee until they were gone.

Mum was on her phone. Excellent! I slid the tomato ketchup and the biscuits into the trolley. When Mum didn't turn round, I went off and got Match Attax (football cards), crisps and humbugs. I slipped these into the trolley too and Mum didn't notice, even though the crisps made a crinkling sound. This was because she was still on her phone, and she stayed on it while she was checking out, which she normally says is rude. I could only assume she was talking to Stephan, or possibly Auntie Mill, who'd been phoning Mum LOADS recently. She lives in a MASSIVE house in Blackheath but was still finding lockdown hard. According to Mum, her roots needed urgent attention (whatever they are) and she'd had to cancel something called Hot Yoga.

Whoever Mum was talking to, she stayed on the phone as she pushed the pushchair towards the exit. I stayed behind her, glancing back until I saw the teenager scoping the checkout lines. I switched to the far side of Mum and stayed there until we were back outside again.

See ya, sucker!

I started to think about the unpacking. I'd got my stuff INTO the shopping, but did Mum actually need to know about it all? The humbugs? The Match Attax? Could I get them OUT without her noticing either? Yes. Just before we got home, I'd go on about rivers, oceans, and waterfalls. Then, after she'd unlocked the door, she'd abandon the pushchair and sprint upstairs to the loo.

Excellent.

But then I had a thought.

I wanted to ask Mum about going to Mrs Stebbings's street. The one she grew up on. I knew what Mum was like. If we went straight home, she'd say no, we'd been out once today already. I decided to ask once we'd got to the top of Egerton Drive – but I frowned.

Where were we?

I'd never been to that supermarket before but I knew where it was. We'd gone down Norman Road and we should have gone back that way. We had started up Norman Road but we must have turned right somewhere. I hadn't noticed. I'd just been plotting, and following. Now I didn't know where we were, which meant that yes, Mum clearly *was* taking me straight to Mrs Stebbings's street! That was great, though she might have let me know. And had she brought my sketch pad?

'Mum?' I said, as we crossed a main road. 'Mum?' I repeated, as we walked past an office building.

Was it the traffic? Mum didn't seem to hear me. I called out again, but then got distracted – by a bus. Or, rather, by someone on it – who seemed to be waving at me. I frowned, but then recognised Semira, the new girl! I just about managed to wave back in time before the bus pulled away, and then turned back to Mum. She STILL had her phone clamped to the side of her head. I knew I shouldn't interrupt when she was talking, but she might have told me where we were going.

'Mum!' I said again.

But still no response! I called out yet again, which FINALLY brought Mum – and the pushchair – to a halt. I put my hands on my hips as Mum turned to face me, swinging the pushchair round. I was about to say, 'Finally!' I was about ask her if she'd brought my sketch pad and my pencils!

But I was distracted by the shopping bags.

The sides were laden with them and I was expecting to see another one, piled up on the seat.

But there was no other shopping bag.

No.

There was . . . a baby.

CHAPTER EIGHTEEN

Horror.

Pure, white, horror.

I couldn't believe it and I stared at two little blue eyes, twinkling from underneath a bobble hat.

As the truth smashed into me.

MUM HAD STOLEN A BABY!

At least I assumed that was the truth. But then I realised – there was no way she'd do that. She's told me SO many times that stealing is wrong – shoplifting especially, though I wasn't sure if stealing a baby at the supermarket actually would be shoplifting, because the baby wouldn't have belonged to the actual shop, would it? Whatever it would have been called, I knew Mum did NOT steal things! No, if she wanted a baby, she'd get one in the normal way (though, thinking about it now, I'm not entirely sure what that is). So, what must have happened – and this was ALMOST AS BAD – is that, instead of stealing the baby, Mum must just have got one by mistake: by taking the wrong pushchair! And that was because she was on her phone! I was about to tell her, but I suddenly realised that, standing behind the pushchair, and looking down at me, WASN'T Mum.

It was someone else.

A woman, but not one I'd ever seen before. So . . .

Ah.

No.

Mum HADN'T taken the wrong pushchair.

I'd taken THE WRONG MUM!

'Can I help you?' the mum said.

Not my mum.

'Er . . .'

'Well?' The Wrong Mum said, with the phone still stuck to her ear.

'Well. Um. Er. No. No, I'm fine.'

'Are you?'

'Yes, I . . . You've . . .'

'Yes?'

'Got the same pushchair as us. So I . . . a little mix-up. No problem.'

'You're okay then?'

'Me?' I said. 'Oh yes. I'm fine. Absolutely.'

'Okay then.' The Wrong Mum smiled. 'Cheerio then.'

And she turned back round and carried on her way. Which left me . . . ?

I had no idea where it left me.

I had no idea where I was!

There were houses, some flats. There was the office building I'd just walked past. There were cars and trucks, another bus swaying past. I turned round and saw more cars at the big junction and then turned back and saw the woman, way on up ahead.

'Wait!' I said. 'Sorry! Can you wait?'

And I started to run forward – because the Wrong Mum had a phone, which meant that she could call the Right Mum. She could tell the Right Mum where I was! Though should I approach the Wrong Mum? She was a stranger. But she had a baby, didn't she? That would be all right. She'd phone and I'd stay there and wait for the Right Mum. Yes, I'd do that. But, as I started to run up to her, the Wrong Mum turned left. She disappeared! I sped up and saw that she'd gone through an entrance, into a green space, a big hedge right ahead of me. There was a path alongside it. I looked one way, before spotting the Wrong Mum going the other. Almost immediately she turned left again, though! I sprinted forward, terrified of losing her, taking the turn too before stopping.

And nearly collapsing on the path in relief.

Because I was standing in Mulberry Park.

The Wrong Mum had just brought the pushchair to a halt – at a bench. She put one shoe on the footrest strap so that the whole thing didn't go over backwards, and got the baby out. The bench was right by a little enclosed playground. It was the playground I'd stood near only the day before, the river beyond it looking normal again now. I sighed, relief washing through me – because I knew Mulberry Park. More importantly, I knew how to get HOME from there.

I took a few deep breaths, thinking for a second about the terror I'd just felt, before my thoughts turned: to Mum. The Right Mum. She'd be tearing her hair out – because I'd vanished. At that very moment she was probably running around screaming my name. Without hesitating any more, I ran up to the Wrong Mum and apologised. I told her what had happened. She was shocked and I could see her thinking of the Right Mum, taking in how terrible she'd be feeling. Without me even asking her, the Wrong Mum grabbed her phone from the bench where she'd put it down. I blurted out Mum's number and she typed it in. I thought she'd just talk to the Right Mum herself but, after thinking about it for a second, she passed the phone to me. I took it and held it near my face as it started to ring. I swallowed. Would Mum be relieved? Would she just be glad that I was safe?

Or would she go totally, and utterly

B

A L

L I

S T

I C

!!!!!!

!!!!!

!!!!

!!!

?

I winced. I crossed my fingers with my free hand, and braced myself. I tried to think of something to say if Mum *was* cross. But I stopped and took a very sharp breath as my eyes were drawn across the path, and then over the little wall.

To the river.

CHAPTER NINETEEN

'Hello? Hello-o? Can I help you?'

That was Mum. On the phone. I was about to tell her that it was NOT my fault! It was hers – because she was covered in so many scarves and masks! I didn't say anything, though – because of what was happening below me.

There was another mum. This one had two kids, who looked to be about four or five. They were dressed in these waterproof all-in-one suits, like miniature frogmen. They had brightly coloured wellies on their feet, and the mum was in wellies too.

And they were all standing in the river.

Why this had drawn my attention, I didn't

know. They were just playing. Exploring. So what? Nevertheless, I stared at them. The two kids were holding on to a low, overhanging branch as they tried to go deeper into the river. Except, they weren't just doing that, were they? They didn't just want to go deeper.

Did they?

No.

They were actually trying to go all the way across the river . . . to the far bank.

So . . . ?

'Hello?' Mum said again, only louder this time.

I turned from the riverbank to the phone. I assured Mum that I was fine and that she didn't need to worry.

'Cym?' she said. 'Is that . . . you?'

'What? Of course!' I said. 'And I'm okay!'

'Good. But . . . how come you're phoning me?'

'What? I wanted you to know that I'm safe.'

'Did you?' Mum seemed confused. 'Then why didn't you just come and tell me? And whose phone are you using?'

I didn't answer that. Instead I said, 'Mum, where ARE you?'

'Where . . . ?' Mum paused and I could hear what sounded like bottles clanking together. 'Just getting something for Auntie Mill.'

'WHAT? You mean you're . . . ?'

'Yes? Cym?'

'STILL IN THE SUPERMARKET?!'

And the answer was yes! Mum was not only still in the supermarket, she was still doing the shopping!

Because she hadn't even noticed that I'd gone!

I was NOT happy. My OWN mother! I would have made it clear to her that she really should start taking her caring responsibilities more seriously! But I didn't want to waste time. I told her what had happened and insisted that I was okay.

'I'm in Mulberry Park,' I explained. 'Near the playground. I'll wait here.'

'All right, but don't . . .'

'Go anywhere near strangers. I won't. Only the Wrong Mum.'

'Who?'

'The lady who lent me the phone. I promise!'

But it was not a promise that I was going to keep.

I did talk to the Wrong Mum. I gave her the phone

back, and thanked her (as she cleaned it with baby wipes). I told her that I knew the park really well and was going to wait there for Mum. I'd just go off and play for a bit. She didn't seem that sure about me leaving her but the baby started to grizzle and she got distracted. She gave it a bottle and it gurgled, and then started flapping its arms up and down, which made its little blue hat fall down over its eyes. It was so cute that, for a second, I sort of wished that Mum *had* stolen it. I thanked the Wrong Mum again, and hurried away.

To the river.

The river – as I've said – runs along the edge of Mulberry Park. The other side is dense with bushes and brambles, with the DLR track behind them. I'd never given any thought to that side of the river because you can't get to it – but now I did. Arriving at the riverbank, I glanced at the two little kids again. The mum was holding their hands because the river was getting too high for their wellies now. She'd given up trying to get them across and was leading them back towards the bank I was on, where they'd gathered all sorts of bits and bobs from the water. There was broken pottery and an old glass bottle, plus some thick, bent nails.

And there were footprints.

Most were from them: different sized wellie prints. There were other prints too, though, which were different. I wasn't completely sure but they looked like they came from trainers. What's more, they weren't going alongside the river like you might expect.

They were going TOWARDS it.

Which made me think of the last time I'd been there.

I took my own trainers off, and then my socks. I rolled up my jeans and waded in. The water was *C~O~L~D* but I kept going – keeping my eyes on the far bank. Halfway across I held on to the low branch to steady myself, and soon the water started to get shallower. There was a flat bit on the far side and cold mud oozed up between my toes before I managed to hop onto a grassy bit, where I paused.

And saw something.

Did I? The bushes *were* dense, so I wasn't exactly sure. I had to get closer. Glancing back to the other side of the river, I checked that the Wrong Mum wasn't watching. Then I moved alongside the bushes and brambles, looking for a way past them. And I saw it! Bending low, I made out a small opening in the foliage. It turned out to be a sort of green tunnel, the grass on the bottom long but flattened down. I crawled in and carried on through it, until I got to the end.

Where I stopped.

And stared.

I'd always assumed that it was just the DLR track on this side of the river. Nothing else. But I was wrong. I was looking at a clearing, littered with old, dry leaves. A big metal box was quite close to me, the sort that you normally see by the side of the road, with electrical stuff in it, probably for the DLR. Beyond that was a big, thick tree whose branches almost completely covered the clearing. Leaning up against it was an old spade, and a hole next to it that someone must have been digging.

Then I saw something else.

It was beyond the tree. I couldn't make it out properly so I crept forward. I emerged from the tunnel and got up to the metal box, where I squatted down on my haunches. And then my eyes nearly BOINGED out of my head.

Because I was looking at a tent.

It was on the far side of the clearing.

And sitting outside it was a girl.

CHAPTER TWENTY

I was jealous. I mean SO jealous. I LOVE camping. Mum and I go to this place in Kent that's great (apart from the stinky showers). It wasn't as exciting as here, though. Camping in a secret wood?! It was so cool – even if the tent wasn't as good as ours. The colours were faded and it was really saggy, with bird poo on it. There were no camping chairs either or a picnic rug – the girl was sitting on an old plastic crate, with some tins of baked beans lying in front of her on a charred bit of ground. That didn't matter, though, and I wondered if Mum would bring me here – until my thoughts turned again.

To my shirt.

The girl was wearing it.

Yes!

I just had to ask for it back. First I had to get her attention, though, and I was about to do that – but the girl stood up. She turned round and I saw something else: a tattered size two football, which made me nod. It was an old one of mine, from the shed! I'd put it outside the house on Sunday. The girl must have taken it as well as my shirt and I soon realised why. I watched as she put her foot on the top of it. I wasn't sure what I'd been expecting but it certainly wasn't for her to flick it up into the air, then kick it up straight with her right foot. She'd done it well, though I was even more impressed when she kicked it up again with her left. I was then gobsmacked when she did, not one knee-up, but two, before following these with two shoulder-ups.

And then a header.

The Super Seven!

It was amazing. She must have seen me do it! She must have copied me! I was so astonished that I lost my balance – and tumbled out from behind the box.

The girl gasped. Then she spun round. Our eyes met, hers going wide as she said, 'Cymbeline?'

What?

How did she know my name?

Of course – Mum had called it out, hadn't she? I nodded, and scrambled to my feet, getting ready to explain – about my shirt. But there was movement from the other side of the tent – which made me realise that there were more than just the two of us in that clearing.

And it emerged.

It stalked right out into the open, and stood next to the girl.

A fox.

No, not A fox. THE fox: the one I'd seen early yesterday morning. The MASSIVE fox. I expected the girl to scream. I expected her to jump away. But she didn't. She didn't even move. She let the fox come right up to her, and stand with its back brushing against her leg. Then she did something that made my mouth drop open.

She stroked it.

I swallowed. I didn't know what to do. But then I did know – because the fox opened its mouth.

And bared its teeth.

And then it leant forward – and began to move.

Forward.

Towards me.

Which is when I, Cymbeline Igloo,

RAN.

CHAPTER TWENTY-ONE

At least, I think I ran. Maybe I flew. In any case, I was through the green tunnel in a millisecond. A millisecond later, I was splashing across the river, waiting for the moment the fox pulled me down by the ankles. Was I was going to end up like the Gingerbread Man? A quarter gone? A half gone? All gone?

It didn't happen. I got across the river without being scoffed, grabbed my socks and trainers, and scrambled up the bank.

And saw Mum.

Mum was just coming into the park – pushing our pushchair. Without even looking back, I climbed over the little wall, just as she reached the Wrong Mum.

The Wrong Mum was still on the bench and must have realised that this was the Right Mum because the two of them started talking – Mum keeping well back – until Mum turned round to me.

'Cym!' she cried, her eyes flashing open. 'You're white as paper. You look . . .'

'Yes, Mum?'

'Terrified, sweetheart.'

And Mum pulled me into a long hug which, I am not embarrassed to admit, I was very happy to get – though not for the reason she thought. Mum kissed the top of my head.

'I'm sorry,' she said, with a huge wince.

Mum let me go then, and studied my face, as if she was trying to make sure that all of me was still there. I told her that she didn't need to apologise and that it was my fault. Mum said that, whatever it was, it didn't matter, and gave me another hug – before asking why my feet were wet. I told her I'd been paddling, and though that made her frown, the Wrong Mum was looking at us, so she accepted it. Mum thanked the Wrong Mum and then gazed down at the baby. It was just dropping off to sleep.

'Oh,' Mum said. 'How lovely. You were like that,

you know, Cymbeline?' Mum laughed and she and the woman chatted, while I frowned – because the little blue hat the kid was wearing actually had a badge on it.

A Millwall badge.

Millwall are Charlton's deadliest rivals! What would Jackie Chapman say? I edged back and pulled Mum's coat for us to go, because this was not only the Wrong Mum.

This was the Wrong Baby, too.

We didn't go to the street where Mrs Stebbings grew up. Mum forgot about it and I didn't remind her. I just wanted to get home. When the door clicked shut behind us, I let out a big sigh. All this time in lockdown wanting to go out, and now I just wanted to be here. Was it getting lost? Or was it the fox? It had scared me SO much, but something else had, too: the scene I'd stumbled across. What was scary about camping, I didn't know, and I wanted to talk to Mum about it, though Mum was all bustling and busy, first unpacking the shopping and then getting the laptop out: for home school.

And it was SO boring.

Honestly, I was beginning to feel like the pet hamster that Lance used to have (Emperor Palpatine) when he ran around on his wheel. Every day was just like the one before. When I'm actually at school, I can feel the week going past. This is because there are different things on different days. P.E. is on Wednesday and Friday. Art is on Tuesday, with Music on Monday. Sometimes there are sports tournaments. Sometimes visitors come in. We had people from the Science Museum once and it was epic.

But Home School NEVER CHANGED. It was also much harder because I couldn't ask questions or look at Mr Ashe's examples on the board. There was also the fact that my mind kept wandering – to that clearing. Again, it made me shiver, though now I knew why: it was the tent. It had made me assume that the girl was there camping with her parents. But who would go on a family camping trip during the week, and in such a tatty tent? And who would casually stroke an actual, real-life, massive fox, not to mention leave old bean tins lying around, if their parents were about? Surely, they'd get told off.

So, was the girl camping there on her own? But that didn't make sense either.

So . . .

I sat back from the screen and swallowed. Was she actually living there?

The idea was too weird.

Living in a scruffy little wood?

In an old tent?

On your own?

Did she have to cook for herself, at that fire? And was that her only way to keep warm at night, without a radiator or a drawer full of jumpers? How did she do all the other things that a house makes easy to do? I didn't want to think about it and, actually, I didn't want to go there again.

I told myself this: that Mum was right. My shirt was . . . well it was just a shirt, wasn't it? It had some names on, but so what? Mum could buy me another one when the season started again. They *are* expensive but she could use the money she'd saved by *not* buying me any ketchup, raspberry ripple or chocolate spread! I could get it signed by the current team. I'm sure I could.

And the girl who actually had my shirt? I decided to just, well, forget about her.

Though it wasn't that easy.

I finished the maths (somehow). Mum was upstairs painting and I stood up because I needed her to take a photo of my work to submit via the online classroom. There was a clicking sound though, from the hall. I went through there and just saw it – on the doormat. It wasn't in an envelope. It was on its own: a folded-up piece of old newspaper. I picked it up, unfolded it, and the simple message seemed to pin me to the spot.

DON'T TELL ON US

PLEASE

I stared at it before yanking the door open, a cold blast of air hitting me in the chest. I jumped out onto the street, but I was too late. I couldn't see anyone. There were just footsteps, pounding away round the corner, which I listened to as raindrops started to blotch the pavement all around me.

'Cymbeline!' Mum called and, after a second, I turned, heading back inside our warm house.

CHAPTER TWENTY-TWO

'Mum,' I said later, as we sat on the Seated Optimal Flop-out Activator watching the news. Words and phrases like 'vaccine testing,' 'Oxford', 'P.P.E.' and 'travel bans' were all making my head spin. There was also a bit on how some people didn't like wearing masks in various places, which I couldn't understand. I'd wear anything to stop other people getting ill.

Even a Millwall shirt.

I think.

Mum turned the volume down.

'I'm sorry about today,' I said. 'And the garden. The hole, I mean.'

Mum sighed. 'Not really your fault. Either thing.

Anyway, we put the grass back down, didn't we? It seems okay. Want to start on the model shelter now?'

I shook my head. 'Maybe later. Can we go to the Stebbings's street? Where they grew up? I need to get my drawing done.'

'Well,' Mum said. 'I want to.'

'Then why can't we?'

'It's weird, Cym.'

'What is?'

'I did call Albert, and he did tell me the name of the street.'

'Great! And?'

'He said he grew up on Thread Street. He said it was near where the DLR station is. There was a silk factory at the end where his and Mrs Stebbings's parents worked. That's how they met.'

'Perfect. So what's the problem?'

'Google Maps hasn't got it.'

'What?'

'It's got Threadneedle Street, but that's up in London where the Bank of England is. There's no Thread Street listed.'

'Did you hear him wrong?'

Mum shrugged. 'Maybe.'

'Can you call him again, to ask?'

'I have, and also to say that we've got some groceries for him. He's not answering the phone. We'll leave it until tomorrow morning, then we'll go round, okay?'

I nodded. 'Okay. But Mum?'

'Yes, love?'

'I was wondering.'

'Go on.' Mum turned to look at me but I shifted away.

'Well, why might someone not live in a flat? Or a house?'

'You mean, if they were homeless?'

I shrugged. 'I think that's what I mean.'

Mum rubbed the side of her face. 'Well, they might have lost their job and got into debt. They might be addicted to things like alcohol. I know that some homeless people have mental health problems.'

'I see. But what if it was . . . ?'

'Yes?'

'A child?'

Mum gave a long sigh. 'I don't know. They could

be running away from problems at home. I'm afraid that some kids' home lives aren't very nice.'

'Couldn't they go to the police? Wouldn't they look after them?'

'They should,' Mum said. 'But the child might not know that. Or be afraid to ask. But, Cym?'

'Yes, Mum?'

'Is there a reason you're asking this?'

'No,' I said, quickly, and I budged up a bit, towards Mum, realising how good it was just to be near to her, feeling the weight of her body next to mine. I couldn't imagine not having her and I saw that sagging tent again. Then I saw Mr Stebbings, how he'd looked when we'd seen him at the allotment and told him what had happened.

'Can you call Mr Stebbings again now?' I asked.

Mum did that, but he still didn't answer. She said he was probably in the greenhouse, or not wanting to use the phone because he was waiting for the hospital to ring. Mum smiled.

'You mustn't worry too much. Mrs Stebbings wouldn't want that. Okay?'

I said okay but I *was* worried – and not just about Mrs Stebbings. Mum reached for the remote control, but I turned to the closed curtains. It was really coming down now, sheets of rain battering the windows so much that it made them rattle.

*

In the morning I woke up feeling pretty good – because Mum hadn't tried to drag me out of bed two hours early again. I wandered downstairs and saw her at the kitchen table – on FaceTime. She drummed her fingers on the table and leaned forwards towards her phone.

'I understand,' she insisted. She looked to the side, and then back in front of her again. 'You have to think hard. I know that. And I know what you have to consider. Of course I do. I just . . .'

Mum stopped and another voice took over. It was Stephan's, though the phone was in front of Mum and I couldn't quite hear what he was saying. Not that I wanted to. This was clearly private and I tried to back out – but Mum realised that I was there. She told Stephan that they'd have to continue this tomorrow and she called me over – to talk to Mabel.

I sighed. Every day, Mabel shows me her latest unicorn picture and demands to know what I think of it. The answer, of course, is that it is EXACTLY

THE SAME AS ALL THE OTHER ONES, though I don't say that. I tell her it's great and then try to escape before I have to take part in her 'bedtime routine'. Mabel sits on her bed and sings her 'Night night, unicorn!' song. I have to join in and it's SO embarrassing, though today I was confused. When I looked down at the phone I could see Mabel, but she wasn't on her bed.

She was on . . . a beach.

Mabel was on a real live sandy beach, with the real sea behind her. And she wasn't in her pyjamas. She was in a T-shirt and shorts and she was running away from the sea, screaming as she dodged the waves. And I realised it wasn't just Mabel. Ellen was there too (her sister, who's my age). I could see her in the background throwing a Frisbee with another girl. It all looked like the most amazing fun and I was dumbstruck, until Mabel ran up to the camera.

'Thimbeline!' she bellowed.

'Hello, Mabel,' I said. 'Are you going to bed?'

'Not yet! Can you see where we are?'

'I think so,' I said, squinting at the little screen.

'Unless that's some background filter like they have on video calls.'

'It's not!' Mabel shrieked. 'It's the real-life filter! I've been swimming! We've had our supper here and everything.'

'But . . .' I started.

'What is it, Thimbeline?' Mabel looked behind her, screamed, and ran off a bit before coming back.

'Well,' I said. 'What about lockdown?!'

'Lockdown?'

'Er, staying at home? Not seeing people?'

'Oh. We got unlocked.'

'What?'

'We can do anything because the virus is under control. It's our prime minister. She's brilliant.'

'So, you don't have to stay at home? You can go out?'

'Yep.'

'And have fun? With other people?'

'Yep.'

'So, you can play FOOTBALL?'

'Of course. I'm getting really good!'

With that, Mabel turned. There was a beach ball

near her and she booted it. The wind sent it back over her head and she laughed, while I stared. This was NOT FAIR. I hadn't seen my friends for WEEKS. Mum was dragging me out at the crack of dawn just to get some space! Meanwhile, Mabel was having such a great time that she hadn't even mentioned UNICORNS yet. I watched as she retrieved the ball, kicked it again, and ran back towards the sea. Then Stephan's face filled the screen.

'She is going to be so upset,' I said. Stephan didn't understand.

'Who?'

'Mabel! And Ellen.'

'Are they? Why, Cym?'

'When you're all allowed to come back,' I explained. 'I mean, having lockdown, here, after all that! They're not going to believe what's hit them.'

I expected Stephan to laugh and agree, but he just smiled. And he didn't quite look at the camera. Nor did he actually reply. Instead, he asked if Mum was still there and I handed her the phone, though she didn't chat to him. She just said 'Bye, then. Talk to you tomorrow maybe,' in the cold voice that I'd heard her use before. Then she hung up and stared out of the window. I did the same. Our garden suddenly looked very small. In fact, it looked tiny. It had never seemed that way to me before and I got an odd, thin feeling, wondering how it would look to someone who had that ginormous beach to run around on. Especially now.

Pretty rubbish, I expect.

I didn't like that feeling, so I turned away and went to get the Weetabix out, after which Mum went on the online classroom to check what I'd be doing that day. I was expecting, of course, more endless hours of hamster-wheel home school – made worse by the knowledge of what Mabel and Ellen were doing at that very second. I dragged my workbooks across the kitchen table towards me and thought of the day when Lance left Emperor Palpatine's cage open. When we found it empty he REALLY cried, though I secretly thought it was a good thing because at least now Palpatine's life wouldn't be quite so dull.

'Maybe he's gone back to the Death Star,' I said, but Lance disagreed. He thought it more likely that his hamster had escaped into the garden – and he was probably right. We never found him but when we got outside, his next-door neighbour's cat was perched on top of their garden wall.

Looking smug.

I geared myself up for more TOTAL boredom, each hour ahead like a separate mountain that I had to trudge to the top of.

But I was in for a surprise.

CHAPTER TWENTY-THREE

Mr Ashe must have been reading my mind!

Instead of school stuff, he'd put a note up. It said that we'd all been working so hard that we needed a break.

We were having the day off!

'Really?' I squealed, jostling Mum to get a look at the screen.

Mum peered closer and said, 'You just have to do "Well-being Activities".'

'What like?'

'Walking in the park or going for a jog.'

'Or . . . watching Star Wars?'

'Not watching Star Wars,' Mum replied. 'How about we go and look for Thread Street? Well?'

I said that was a great idea, and I went to get a sketch pad. It wasn't the beach, quite, but at least we'd be outside, doing something different.

Mum locked up the house and we walked up towards the allotments. I was pleased to see that she seemed okay. She didn't even make us cross the road when a dog walker approached. We just stepped to the side.

She was right, though – we looked everywhere but, just as Google Maps said, there was no Thread Street. It was really confusing, since we were definitely in the right place. Mum pointed to the little alley that we'd walked along the day before yesterday. I'd never even realised that it had a name.

'Silk Mills Passage,' I said, staring up at the sign. 'So we must be getting warm. Where's the silk mill, though?'

Mum put her hands on her hips and turned her head from side to side. She waited for the noise of a DLR train to subside, and said, 'It must have been demolished, especially if the factory closed. A lot of stuff was knocked down after the war.'

'But you can't knock a street down,' I argued. 'Can you?'

Mum agreed that this would be very unlikely. After walking about a bit more – and going on Google Maps again – she shrugged. 'I think we'll just have to go round to see Albert. We'll give him the groceries and ask him. Maybe I did get the name wrong.'

'But we won't tell him why we want to know,' I insisted. 'My picture HAS to be a surprise for Mrs Stebbings.'

Mum agreed and we walked up to the main road.

We crossed at the pelican crossing. We walked up Morpeth Hill and Mum rang the Stebbings's doorbell. When there was no reply, she peered through the window again, like she had the other morning. Then she looked for somewhere to leave the bag of food. The only place was the greenhouse and she slid the door open. She moved the bag forward but stopped and stood up straighter.

'Oh, look,' she said. 'Look at that, Cym.'

I came up behind Mum. She stood aside and there, just inside the greenhouse door, were SIX more bags of food. They must have been brought by more people from our school – all of whom cared enough to come. Mum tilted her head to the side, though I sighed. Yes, it was great to see, but if only Mrs Stebbings could see it too. Why do we leave it until people aren't there to show how much we care for them? I decided to change that. The next time I saw Veronique, I would tell her how much it means to me that, in normal times, she lets me copy her homework. I'd do the same with Lance, telling him how much I love playing Subbuteo with him (because I'm a teensy bit better, which means I normally win). Yes, I would tell him that, though . . .

THERE WAS LANCE!

Lance was walking down the hill with his dad!

'LANCE!' I bellowed.

Lance's dad also had a bag of food in his hand. He held a hand up to wave, but Lance came sprinting down. When his dad caught up, Mum pointed into the greenhouse.

'I should have asked,' Lance's dad said. 'No bother. I can take the perishable stuff back home. But . . .' His dad turned towards the house. 'Albert's not in then?'

Mum said no. The two of them started to chat (in a socially distanced way) and I turned to Lance. He didn't have a bag of food in his hand. He had something else, something that – I kid you not – made my mouth water.

A football.

I stared at it. Both Lance and I started to edge away, but then Mum saw us. I bit my lip and looked up at her.

'Please,' I whispered.

Mum started to speak but I stopped her.

'We'll stay two metres apart. PLEASE!'

I crossed my fingers and stayed really still as Mum glanced at Lance's dad. Then, incredibly, she nodded – and Lance and I were OFF. Lance put the ball down but I pointed up the hill, where I knew there was a flat bit. We ran up there, and stood opposite each other: not on the online classroom or on Zoom, but in person. I'd been SO looking forward to this, and to start with I just grinned.

But it was weird: neither of us knew what to say. I mean, what DO you say to your best friend? Words normally just blurt themselves out, because we're connected to each other. We're either together or, if not, doing the same things. When we do see each other, we compare notes, but how could we? I didn't really know what Lance had been up to. He didn't know what I'd been doing. Could I tell him about seeing the mist along the river? The girl? It would take too long. There was so much to say and ask that it was hard to know where to start. I realised that it would probably be easier to talk to Semira, the new girl, because at least I'd be able to give her some info about the school and stuff. In contrast, Lance and I just stood there. It made me wonder if this was the same for friends everywhere. Did everyone feel the way I did? Scared that they might lose their friends? Was lockdown doing this to everyone?

But then I realised something.

Lance and I had something that was far more important to us than talking could ever be!

And he was holding it!

Lance dropped the football to the floor. When it was still, we both stared at it. Then Lance moved his foot forward and, like an unleashed puppy, the football dashed forward. My right foot didn't need telling – it reached out and trapped it. And the feeling? It was like there was a very small angel standing on the top of my big toe. It was just as good when I kicked the ball back to Lance, who had so much glee on his face that he looked a bit frantic. He passed the ball back and I trapped it again, the angel seeming to sigh with happiness. It was so great, though then Lance's gaze moved from the ball to something over my shoulder.

'Vi!' he shouted.

I turned behind me. Vi Delap had come too – with her dad. He also had a food bag, which made me shake my head. Vi had her hair down, which she normally doesn't at school. It made her look really grown up, and she also looked taller. Mum had said I'd grown recently but Vi REALLY had, something that not seeing her for a long while had made me notice. And I didn't like it. It was as if I'd missed some time, some of my life, as if some pages had been torn out of it. Pages I'd never get to read. It made me think about everyone else in my class and I wondered if, when we DID go back, we would even really know each other. It scared me, but I didn't get much time to think about it because Vi came rushing down.

Though not to play football with us.

'Look!' she screamed.

Vi had a phone in her hand. I thought she was just showing us that and I was about to be very jealous (Mum says no to me getting one yet). It wasn't that, though. She was on the internet and I recognised the site.

'I was looking for when the trials are,' Vi explained. Vi and Daisy had been asked to try out for the Charlton girls' team at the end of the season. It had nothing to do with that, though. Vi was in 'Latest News' and she scrolled down to a headline which said:

'CORONAVIRUS AND THE CHARLTON FAMILY.'

Vi clicked on it. It wasn't a long article, just going on a bit about how all the staff and players at Charlton were thinking of their fans who might be affected by Covid-19. I couldn't understand why Vi was showing it to us until she scrolled down – to a video.

Of Jackie Chapman!

There he was: the greatest captain Charlton had ever known. Vi clicked and he began to speak, saying the same sorts of things that the article had, but then he started to mention actual names.

And the last fan he talked about was Eileen Stebbings!

Which was our Mrs Stebbings!

And he didn't just say her name. Jackie Chapman said that she was the dinner lady at our school – St Saviour's in Blackheath. He said that Mrs Stebbings was the most committed fan in the whole club family, and at the end of the video a really determined look came over his face and he said, 'Get well soon, Eileen.' He put both thumbs up to the camera. 'Your club and your school both need you.'

'Wow,' Lance said.

The video ended and Vi let the phone fall to her side.

'Jackie Chapman,' Lance said under his breath. 'Was. Just. Speaking. About. Our. Dinner. Lady.'

'She has to see this,' I whispered. 'It'll . . .'

'Mean so much to her,' Vi went on. 'And Mr Stebbings has to see it too.'

'Yes!' I said. 'Yes. He absolutely HAS to. But . . .'

I hissed out a sigh and spun round, to the (now) three adults who were all outside the Stebbings's house. I looked at the blank windows in front of them, and the open greenhouse door, and I was about to sigh again – when it came to me.

I broke away from Lance and Vi. I sprinted down to Mum and grabbed her hand.

'I know where he is!' I said.

CHAPTER TWENTY-FOUR

Ten minutes later we were in the car. We drove towards the allotments, though we didn't stop there. We went on past the closed gates, and then on past the Tesco. We crossed the big roundabout and then drove alongside the shopping centre, where Mum drags me for haircuts and eye tests.

Then we were there.

Mum parked and we got out, hurrying through the other stationary cars until we saw it.

The Morris Minor.

'Yes!' I said.

I half expected Mr Stebbings to be inside. I really wanted him to be, in fact, because I'd loaded the website up on Mum's phone. He would LOVE it and

Mrs Stebbings would too – if we could just find a way to show it to her. The Morris Minor was empty, though, so we carried on, round past a line of ambulances to the front.

Of the hospital. Lewisham Hospital.

Where I swallowed.

I've been to Lewisham Hospital A LOT, with twists, sprains, broken bits, nearly broken bits, rashes, embarrassing rashes, really embarrassing rashes, vomiting, swallowing the wrong thing and not vomiting; you name it. Honestly, I could give you a guided tour. My most recent visit was just before lockdown, when I tripped over and smashed Mabel's unicorn piggy bank. Mum took me in to get the unicorn's horn removed from my left ear. It had seemed like its normal self, then, though today it was anything but.

It looked scary.

Normally, people just wander in and out of Lewisham Hospital, chatting on phones or talking to each other. Not now though. The entrance was blocked off with tape. Nurses were standing behind it, or at least I presumed that's what they were. They were wearing these massive suits like astronauts do. They were directing people into different lanes, marked out by the tape, though not everyone was trying to get inside. Some were just standing behind the tape, not moving.

And one of them was Mr Stebbings.

Who was staring up at the hospital.

Mr Stebbings had a suit on, and a tie, the wind flicking at his glossy white hair. He looked small, and cold. Most of all, alone. I blinked at him and swallowed, and Mum let out a long sigh.

'Albert?' she said.

Mr Stebbings didn't hear Mum at first. She tried again and he turned, a look of surprise on his face. He drew away from us, though he wasn't being rude – it was so we'd be safe. He tried to smile and I was about to show him Mum's phone. But something was wrong. I could just tell. Mum could, too. She asked if he'd had any news.

'Yes.' Mr Stebbings coughed. 'They . . . called me this morning.'

'And?' Mum made to step forward but stopped herself. 'Albert?'

Mr Stebbings hesitated and then looked down at the floor. 'She's gone into the ICU,' he said.

CHAPTER TWENTY-FIVE

I looked from Mum to Mr Stebbings, and then back to Mum again. 'What is that?' I said, with a voice that didn't sound like mine. 'Mum? What is the ICU?'

'It means Intensive Care,' Mum said. 'The Intensive Care Unit.'

I took that in. 'Is that . . . bad?'

Mum looked down at me. 'Well, they'll be keeping a really close eye on Mrs Stebbings now. Sort of like, one on one. Did they say anything else, Albert?'

'Just that she'd had a bad night. Her breathing.'

'Oh,' I said, and it must have sounded a bit shaky because Mr Stebbings turned to me. 'She's a fighter though, Cymbeline. Lived through the Blitz, she did.'

'I know,' I said, and I did. Mrs Stebbings was strong.

She wasn't very tall but, as a person, she was so big. 'But she needs to know something.'

'What's that?'

'Well, that people are thinking of her. And not just any old people, either.'

And I stepped forward to show Mr Stebbings the video.

It wasn't easy. Mr Stebbings didn't want us to go anywhere near him. He told us that he shouldn't have been there. He should have been at home, on his own, even though he'd had a test that had shown that he himself didn't have coronavirus. I had to put the phone down on the post that the tape was tied to, and move away while Mr Stebbings watched it. It sort of crumpled him. He took a breath and moved his head a bit, before looking back up at the hospital again. He was trying to picture her. Mrs Stebbings. He was trying to imagine her there, inside. Eventually he turned to me.

'She'll love that,' he said.

'I know. It's not just Jackie Chapman either. It won't be as amazing for her, but we're all doing something too.'

Mr Stebbings blinked. 'Who is?'

'My class.' And I told him about our projects on World War Two: how they were all for Mrs Stebbings.

'What?'

'We're all doing something she'll be interested in,' I explained. 'Vi's doing food. Rationing and stuff. Veronique's doing music. She's learning some songs. Lance and Billy are doing Charlton in the war. We're going to make her a video of it all.'

'That's . . . lovely. Was it . . . your idea?'

'That doesn't matter.'

'But it was, wasn't it?'

Quickly, I nodded.

'And what are you doing?'

'Me? I want it to be a surprise, but you lived on Thread Street, didn't you? In the war. Mum told me. Is that right?'

Mr Stebbings said it was.

'Near the allotments?'

'Near enough. We lived at number nine. It was a cul-de-sac with the factory wall at the end. That's gone now, of course. Both my parents worked there.'

'What did the factory make?'

'Well, before the war it made all the fancy braid you see on uniforms. For admirals and the like. The king even. My old mum used to love it when he was in the newspaper. Then it made normal uniforms. Mum was a machinist. Dad worked in the warehouse. It was all horses when he started.'

'And what about Mrs Stebbings?'

Mr Stebbings's face lit up. 'She moved in when I was about ten I'd say. Number twenty-two. She was only five or six.'

'What was she like?'

Mr Stebbings laughed. 'Cheeky! Used to follow me about all day. I thought she was a right little pest. I just wanted to hang out with my mates, see. Checking out the bomb sites. Playing football. She insisted on joining in, which girls didn't do back then.'

'Was she any good?'

'At football? Well, she was fierce, I can tell you. Take your shin off, if you weren't careful. And she could boot it! One time she gave it a right old dig and it broke the Roberts's front window. Went straight through! What a crash it made! Ma Roberts was a right dragon and she came steaming out into the street. I can see her now, fists on her hips like the FA Cup. Little Eileen was terrified. She turned tail and scarpered. While I . . .'

Mr Stebbings paused, and took a breath, pressing his mouth closed as the memory flooded into him.

'Yes?' I said.

'Well, I took the blame, didn't I? Said it were me. And Eileen . . .'

Again Mr Stebbings stopped speaking. This time it was Mum who prompted him. 'Yes, Albert?'

'Well, she said that's what did it.'

'Did what?'

'She was hiding behind one of the factory vans, Eileen was. She saw Ma Roberts giving me what for, and me not letting on. And she went home and told her mum.'

'What did she tell her, Albert?'

'Well, she were only little still, but she told her that she'd found her husband. She wasn't going to marry anyone else but Albert Stebbings. Best thing I ever did, that was, even though Ma Roberts gave me a right old walloping. Yep. Best thing ever.'

Mr Stebbings turned away then, and we watched him walk towards a lamp post, which he held on to with one hand. I saw him begin to shake and it was scary. You don't see adults cry very often. When you do, it seems to mean more than when children do it.

It completely stopped me and I was very still until Mr Stebbings took out a handkerchief and wiped his eyes. He came back and apologised but Mum said he didn't have to. It was natural. She felt like crying too.

'It's just her in there alone,' Mr Stebbings said. 'That's what I can't stand. Me being out here. Not sitting with her, telling her she'll be all right. Telling her how many people are pulling for her. So that video you're making, Cym . . . Fantastic.'

'We can get one of the nurses to show it to her,' I said. 'I bet we can.'

'That would be great. And, Cymbeline?'

'Yes?'

'Will you be the one to introduce it?'

'Me?'

'Yes. She's got a soft spot for you. She says you care about people. She'd love it if you told her what it was all about.'

'Then I will,' I said.

'Great.' Mr Stebbings nodded, and then seemed to have an idea. He nodded again and actually grinned, his eyes lighting up as he held up a finger to me. 'And why don't you wear your shirt?'

I stared at him. 'My . . . ?'

'Shirt! Your special one? The one you brought into school. She went on about that for weeks. Signed by the players! Given to you by Jackie Chapman! Why don't you wear that in the video, Cym?'

CHAPTER TWENTY-SIX

We left Mr Stebbings there. We didn't want to. Mum tried to persuade him to go home. She told him about all the food that people had left.

'For me?' he said. 'But why would they?'

'Because they care, Albert. Lots of people do.'

'Well, it's very kind. I'll pick it up later.'

'Will you? You won't stay here all night?'

Mr Stebbings shook his head. 'I promise. I'll go home in a bit, but for now . . . I'll stay. She knows I'm here. I asked one of the nurses to tell her. And she'd know anyway. She just would. But thanks for coming, you two. I can't tell you how much it means. Can't wait to see that film you're making, Cymbeline.'

Mr Stebbings turned to the big building in front of

us and for a second we did too – and I pictured Mrs Stebbings inside. Then I pictured all the people in there with coronavirus, who all had families: husbands or wives, sons or daughters, mums and dads who were worried about them. It made me realise something. There was a couple, twenty yards away, both about the same age as Mum. They'd been there when we'd arrived, and they hadn't moved. The man's arm was round the woman's shoulders, her arm around his waist. Like Mr Stebbings, they were staring at the hospital too.

'Come on, Cym,' Mum said.

When we got into the car, I expected Mum to drive away but instead she reached over to hold my hand.

'I'm sorry,' she said.

'Sorry?'

Mum sighed. 'About your shirt. Once again, I'm so sorry. I'll order you a new one as soon as we get back. It won't be the same though, will it?'

I didn't answer for a second. Mum was right, but what she didn't know was that I knew where the original shirt was. And now I knew I had no choice. I *had* to get it back. That place on the other side of the river was pretty scary, but so what? All sorts of things could be scary, like going into hospital or starting a new school. Even going to the shops. I didn't care: I HAD to get the shirt back, and not just for the presentation. I would wear it in the film, but after that I'd wrap it up and I'd bring it back here. And then, somehow, SOME way, I'd get the shirt inside.

And give it to Mrs Stebbings.

I nearly told Mum then – about the girl. I put my hand in my pocket, though, and felt the note, which I'd picked up from the letterbox yesterday and stuffed in there.

DON'T TELL ON US

PLEASE

The girl wouldn't have put it through our door unless there was a really good reason for it. I also knew that Mum wouldn't just leave the girl alone, if she knew what she was doing. So, I had to get back to Mulberry Park.

AND I had to get back there on my own.

But how?

I tried when we were back home. I asked Mum if

she had any letters to post, hoping she'd let me go off to the letterbox on my own. She said yes, but then said they weren't urgent and she'd take them tomorrow. My next idea was the allotment.

'Do you think it's all right?' I asked.

'I expect so,' Mum replied. 'Why?'

'Mr Stebbings can't go down there, can he?'

'No, but he only goes once a week anyway.'

'But did he shut the place up properly last time? The shed, for instance?'

'I imagine so.'

'He was pretty upset. He might have forgotten. Why don't I check? You have a cup of tea. I won't be long.'

But Mum wouldn't let me. Now that I'd put the doubt in her head, she had to go herself. It was all fine, of course. While she checked the locks, I stared at the wall that the girl had jumped over and pictured the raspberries tumbling out of her baseball cap. Then I pictured those empty baked-bean tins. She hadn't been stealing raspberries to be naughty, had she? She'd done it for something to eat. I sighed and, once again, nearly told Mum about her. But I shook my head. I had to get to see her first, though how? I wasn't just locked down by lockdown, was I? I was also locked down by being me. Everything I ever did was with the complete knowledge of my mum, who knew where I was at every single second of my life.

Or did she?

I swallowed because that wasn't quite true. And it gave me another idea. I knew how I could get to Mulberry Park on my own. First, I'd have to wait until Mum was asleep. Then I'd have to sneak downstairs and out of the house. I'd have to walk down the road, on my own – in the dark! Then I'd have to cross the bridge, where people sometimes sit, drinking beer and smoking, using words that make Mum's face go tight. If I managed to do that, I'd have to walk through the park, which would be really dark, and empty, though nowhere near as bad as the river. I'd have to cross it. I'd have to crawl through the tunnel into the clearing, which would be pitch black. I'd have to walk towards the tent, the girl inside it probably just as scared as I was, especially if she heard someone coming. And it wouldn't just be her, would it? There would be that fox, which would see me long before I would ever be able to see it.

I swallowed and shook my head, as the whole thing

played out through my mind like some terrible dream. It was ABSOLUTELY terrifying, but made worse by a simple fact. Yes, it was scary, much scarier than I'd imagined. In fact, it was scarier than anything else I could actually think of.

But I was still going to have to do it.

For Mrs Stebbings.

And every single person who cared about her.

CHAPTER TWENTY-SEVEN

'Mum,' I said (later on). She was looking in the freezer. 'You didn't do Bobby Bunns this morning.'

'Oh. No. I . . . didn't feel like it.'

'Was it because of what you were talking to Stephan about?' I remembered her tone, and how she'd practically hung up on him.

'What?' Mum looked alarmed. 'No.'

'Is everything all right with Stephan?'

'Of course. We've just . . .'

'Yes, Mum?'

Mum shut the freezer door. 'Got things to work through.'

'I see. But why don't you do Bobby Bunns now?

'Now?'

'On Catch-up. It'd be good for you. It might help take your mind off things.'

Mum thought about it and then nodded. She went to get changed. Then she jumped up and down in front of the TV. When I joined in, Mum looked surprised, though she didn't say anything.

'Are you tired?' I asked, once she'd finished.

'You bet,' she panted, waving a hand at her face.

'Right,' I said.

Mum trudged upstairs for a shower and then carried on with supper. I went outside and pretended to do kick-ups, though after five minutes I stopped – and nosed around in the shed.

'You okay, Cym?'

Mum had popped her head out of the kitchen window. 'Yes,' I said, putting my hands behind my back. In them was a torch. 'I'm fine. What's for supper?'

The answer to that was – you've guessed it – Fishless Fish Fingers. Not that this bothered me because I'd beaten that teenager to the last bottle of ketchup, hadn't I? I nodded, remembering my total triumph, and imagined covering the FFFs in thick red gloop. But then I realised: I'd slipped the ketchup into the wrong trolley!

That Millwall baby had my ketchup!

And my Match Attax!

I screwed my eyes up in frustration and when I opened them again there were four grey sticks on my plate, which didn't look like food so much as badly made Jenga bricks. I didn't care though. I had more important things to think about. I forced two down and gave a massive yawn.

'Bobby Bunns. He's really worn me out. I'm going to bed early tonight. What about you, Mum?'

'Sounds like a plan. I won't be long behind you.'

Only she was.

I went to bed with no fuss, figuring that the sooner Mum thought I was asleep, the sooner she'd go to sleep too, and the sooner I could get to Mulberry Park – making it less scary. I lay under my duvet (fully dressed) and listened. The TV stayed on for ages, though, and then her phone rang. After that she went around the house, opening and shutting cupboards. The washing machine started up. Even after she'd cleaned her teeth and gone into her bedroom, I could still hear her. When I crept onto the landing, I saw a light beneath her bedroom door. I guessed she was working on her river painting and I should have been pleased because painting helps make her feel calmer. It helps her deal with things. I so wanted her to stop though – AND GO TO SLEEP – and when I heard her door open, I thought she was finally about to do it. I was expecting her to come in and check on me, so I lay down flat, with my eyes closed, the duvet right up to my chin.

But her footsteps went past.

It was the washing machine. It was beeping, which meant it must have finished. I thought Mum would just to go down and turn it off, but I heard her getting the drying rack out from under the stairs! Why hanging the washing up couldn't wait until the morning I didn't know, but I listened as she did it. Then she came up the stairs again, but she still didn't come in. Instead, she shuffled outside my door, hanging the stuff that wouldn't fit on the rack over the banisters. That had to be it, though, surely! I closed my eyes again, certain that she'd come in, my right hand gripping the torch. I stared into the swirly darkness on the inside of my eyelids, picturing an even darker darkness in Mulberry Park. Then I wondered how long should I leave it after she'd kissed me goodnight.

Five minutes?

Ten?

Fifteen maybe?

I decided on fifteen and shifted over a bit to wait.

And then . . .

And then . . .

And then . . .

CHAPTER TWENTY-EIGHT

I woke up.

IN THE MORNING!!!

CHAPTER TWENTY-NINE

I did. I just opened my eyes and . . . light was trying to barge its way through my curtains! And Mum was walking in. She had an armful of washing – from the drying rack. After stepping round my Subbuteo pitch, she set it down on the end of my bed. I stared at her, SO cross with myself. And Bobby Bunns. He really had tired me out, hadn't he? I banged my fists against my head as Mum stared at me. Then she pulled my duvet back.

'Cym?' she said. 'What's this?' She held up the torch. 'And why are you dressed already?'

'Oh.' I shook my head and pushed myself upright. 'Sleep dressing.'

'What?'

'It's a thing, apparently. Lance told me. Something to do with lockdown.'

'I see. I'll look it up. But . . .'

'Mum?'

'I've got some news on that.'

I pushed some sleep out of my eye. 'On what?'

Mum sat on the edge of my bed. 'On lockdown.' She smiled. 'It's been hard on you, hasn't it? Being stuck at home? And home learning. Let's face it, you're not a natural, are you?'

I shrugged. 'Not really. But . . . ?'

'Cym.' Mum put a hand on my arm. 'I got a call last night.'

'From Mr Stebbings?'

'No, love. From school. My school.' Mum meant the school she taught in, though she was only part-time. She hadn't been there because of the pandemic.

'And?' I said.

'Some staff have gone on sick leave.'

'With coronavirus?'

'Yes, and another bug. They're very short-staffed. So . . .'

'So?'

'They've asked me to cover.'

'To . . . ?'

'Go in. I'm very nervous about it, but they're desperate. So I've said yes. Which means . . .'

'What?' I said, and I didn't understand until I looked again at the clean washing that Mum was now sitting next to. On the top of the pile was a pair of trousers: grey trousers. There was a white polo-shirt too, and a red jumper.

With the St Saviour's logo on.

Which meant that, while almost every other kid in the entire country was at home, I, Cymbeline Igloo, would be going to SCHOOL!

'It's only for one day,' Mum assured me, as my mouth dropped open. 'They'll be fine on Friday apparently, but come on. We don't have much time.'

And we didn't.

Not that we were late, but it had been ages since we'd actually had to get out the house for something. It felt weird, like we were on some fast-moving conveyor belt. After cursing myself again for falling asleep, I hurried downstairs. I wanted to hit the S.O.F.A. but I couldn't. Two Weetabix were already sitting in a bowl, waiting for the milk. I poured it on and spooned them down, and Mum told me to go upstairs to do my teeth. I did, got re-dressed, let Mum attack me with the Instrument of Parental Torture (hairbrush) and that was it.

Done.

Sorted.

Finished.

We were through the door, like the house had actually booted us out of it. Mum locked up, reached into her bag, and then pointed across the road.

'BLEEP,' said our car, as it unlocked.

We were going in the car because Mum's school is quite a long way away, in a place called Lee. She was going to drop me off first and then go on there. I got in and pulled my safety belt on, feeling weird. The first thing was the car, which we'd hardly used during lockdown. It didn't feel quite like it belonged to us. Then there was the fact that I didn't know how to feel. Miserable? Or pleased? I didn't know. I decided it depended on who would be at school with me and I thought about Lance. No. His dad does computer work and was looking after him at home. Veronique was a no, too, because her mum's a musician who wasn't able to perform. She could stay at home too. I thought about Billy, but his mum doesn't go out to work, so what about the others, whose parents I didn't know so well? There was Daisy, and Vi. We could talk tactics. We could practise the Super Seven. Then I thought about the other kids in my year and even the kids in the years below. I could play football with them at lunchtime, be sort of like their mentor, teaching them stuff.

I decided that it would be fine, and by the time Mum dropped me off at the top of the steps, I was actually pleased about being there. I can't really describe it properly, but the school looked really solid. Real. I walked down the steps, wondering who I'd see at the bottom, but not really caring, actually. I do have my main friends, but there's nobody in my class I don't really like.

But no one was at the bottom of the steps.

I stared up the road, and then through the school gates – but the only person I could see was Mrs Robinson (who I'd had in Year Three, and pushed in the pond). Mrs Robinson opened the gate for me and, after I'd said goodbye to Mum, I walked through to her.

'Who else is here?' I asked.

Mrs Robinson was about to reply, but she couldn't;

a dad was walking down the road with a Reception kid in his arms, who was bawling his head off. He didn't stop crying when he saw Mrs Robinson – she is not what you'd call the smiliest of teachers. He only quietened down when Mrs Robinson said that I'd see him into his classroom.

I was annoyed because I wanted to know who else was going to be there with me. I did it, though, staring at the walls as I walked past them. The whole place looked completely familiar but entirely alien at the same time. I squinted at one of the paintings, up above the coats. The edges were a bit curled over, though that's not why it had caught my attention. It was one of mine, but it seemed so totally separate from me – like a much younger version of me had done it. I didn't like looking at it for some reason, so I turned away.

'Come on,' I said to the Reception kid. 'It'll be all right.'

The kid nodded and followed me into the Reception classroom. There were ten kids in there already, some from Reception, the rest from Year One and Year Two. Miss Phillips was in charge of them, and she smiled when she saw me in the doorway.

'Just stay there, if you would, Cymbeline,' she said. 'You're not in this bubble.'

'Where will I be, then?'

'You're in Year Six, with all of Key Stage Two. Okay?'

I nodded and watched the Reception kid run off towards one of his friends, who held her arms out to give him a hug. He was all right now, and I was sure I would be, too.

I turned round, retraced my steps towards my painting, and then headed up the stairs. The stairs were quiet, though not as quiet as the Year Six classroom I was faced with when I pushed the door open.

Unlike the rooms I'd passed, the chairs were down, but the classroom was completely empty. It made me frown. Miss Phillips must have got it wrong. Key Stage Two had to be somewhere else.

Unless . . .

I thought about it, and looked at the seats closest to me.

Maybe I WAS Key Stage Two.

I put my hands on my hips and stared around the

room. Was I going to be here on my own? Just me – and Mr Ashe? Even though I really liked him, that would be STRANGE. I swallowed, relieved to hear the door opening behind me. Vi? Daisy? Danny? No: it was Mrs Robinson.

'Don't look so worried, Cymbeline.'

'I'm not,' I said. 'I was just wondering.'

'Yes?'

'If there's going to be . . .'

'Anyone else?' Mrs Robinson strolled past me as the door swung shut. 'There is.'

'Great. Who else is coming in? From my year, I mean?'

'Well, there's . . . Ah!'

Mrs Robinson stopped speaking because there were footsteps – on the stairs. I stared at the now-closed door and crossed my fingers. Maybe Lance's dad had been called into a meeting or something. But it wasn't him. I knew that because Lance never stops outside – he just barges in. Whoever was outside had come to a complete halt and was standing outside the door.

'Come in!' Mrs Robinson called.

But nothing happened.

Mrs Robinson had to call out a second time. Only then, and very slowly, did the door begin to swing open. It didn't come all the way, though, so Mrs Robinson reached out and pulled the handle; and I was looking at a girl.

The girl was my height, and wearing a very new-looking school uniform. Was she in the year below? I wasn't sure and I just stared at her for a moment until Mrs Robinson spoke.

'This is Cymbeline,' she said, too loudly.

'Hello,' the girl replied.

'Great. And, Cymbeline,' Mrs Robinson went on, 'this is Semira.'

Semira! Of course. The new girl. I hadn't recognised her immediately because we hadn't met in person yet, and when I'd seen her on video calls and on the bus, her hair had been in two big puffs. Now it was in tight braids. I nodded 'Hi' and stared past her into the corridor – listening out for more footsteps.

But there were no footsteps. I turned to Mrs Robinson.

'Is this it?' I asked.

Mrs Robinson frowned. 'It?'

'Sorry. I just mean, is no one else coming?'

'Today? No. It's just you two.'

'Just . . . ?'

Mrs Robinson raised her eyebrows at me. 'Just, Cymbeline . . . ?'

'Oh. I mean, yeah, great.'

Mrs Robinson sucked her cheeks in and eyed me. 'Good. Now, you've ten minutes before we need to start. Cymbeline, make Semira feel at home while I sort a few things out. Take a seat. I'll be back in a jiffy.'

Mrs Robinson gave me what I can only describe as a 'significant' look, and walked out. Which left the new girl and me.

Semira gave me a quick, shy smile. She edged past me and, very gingerly, pulled out one of the chairs from the nearest table. She perched on the edge of it as I pulled one out too. After telling myself, again, that it didn't matter that none of my really close friends were there, I attempted to do what Mrs Robinson had said: to make Semira feel at home.

'Er . . .' I said, which wasn't a particularly good start, I admit. Semira was eager to answer, though.

'Yes?' she said, her eyes opening wide as they searched out mine. I opened my mouth but shut it again, because talking to Semira wasn't going to be as easy as I'd first thought. I was relieved when Semira nodded to herself.

'Cymbeline,' she said, trying the word out like a new sweet. 'That means you're . . . Cym?'

I nodded 'Yeah. No one calls me Cymbeline. Except teachers. And my mum, when she's being serious. And Auntie Mill. And some doctors, though not the ones I know. But . . . "Semira"?'

'Yes?' Semira said.

'Do people shorten that?'

'To what?'

'I dunno. Er. Sem?'

I had no idea why I said that, and Semira clearly didn't know either.

'No,' she said.

'Right. Is this your first day coming in, too?'

'Yes. My mum got offered a job so she can't look after me.'

'And you can't use her mobile phone, either?'

'Right,' Semira said.

I nodded again. Then smiled. Then there was another silence, which was even longer than the first one. I looked at Semira. Semira looked at me. Then we both did that again as I searched desperately for something to say. Eventually I just blurted out:

'You don't support Millwall, do you?'

The words seemed to hang around in the room for a bit, until Semira frowned. 'What's Millwall?' she said.

'Oh. It's a football team. So they claim.'

'Ah. In that case, no, I don't support them.'

'Charlton then?'

'Is that another . . . ?'

'Football team? Yes. They are absolutely . . .'

'Then no.' Semira cut me off. 'I don't. I don't like football.'

'You don't . . .' GREAT. I tried not to sigh. Or think of breaktime. Just us. A bit more silence happened, and then a bit more, so I said, 'What do you like, then?'

'Er . . .'

'Star Wars, perhaps?'

Semira thought about it. 'Is that the one with the two robots who can't go very fast?'

'Yes!'

Semira grimaced.

'What?' I said. 'You . . . don't like it?'

'Well, I couldn't understand why you'd use those shiny sword things . . .'

'Lightsabres!'

'Or those laser beams that are so easy to dodge out the way. In the future, you'd think they would have thought of that.'

'What? No! The thing is . . .' And I was about to explain, when Semira shook her head.

'And I don't like fighting much anyway.'

'Oh.' I looked around the room for a bit and tried not to sigh. 'I see. Not football then, or Star Wars.'

'I like reading,' Semira said. 'Do you?'

'Sometimes.'

'What are you reading now?'

'My Charlton annual. It's mostly about football. Before that I read . . .'

'Yes?'

'A book about Star Wars.'

'Oh.' Semira tried to smile again, but it didn't really work. She looked down at her knee. 'Well, I don't just like reading.'

'Cool! What else do you like? I'm sure we've got something in common!'

'Maps,' Semira said.

I looked at her. 'Did you say . . . ?'

'Maps. Making them. Looking at them.'

'Riiiiiiight,' I said.

'But my favourite thing is this,' Semira said, and she turned to her bag, which was sitting on her knee. She loosened a toggle at the top, while I crossed my fingers. Was it going to be some Top Trumps? A Transformer? What if it was a Nintendo Switch? That would be epic!

What Semira drew out, however, was some bobbly yellow material and a ball of wool, with two spikes poking out.

Which I blinked at.

'What's that?' I asked.

'It's knitting,' Semira said.

I took that in. 'Knitting?'

'My mum's pregnant. I'm making a little hatty for the baby.'

'A little . . . ? Fabulous. That's . . . really something.'

'It is! Do you . . . ?'

'What?'

'Want to have a go?'

'Do I . . . ?'

'Want to have a go at knitting?'

'Er . . .'

'I'll show you what to do. Look.'

I tried to tell Semira that she really didn't need to bother, but she shuffled her chair forward. She spread the material out a bit and the spikes began to move. Then she pushed the material over to me.

I sat back. 'I'm okay, actually.'

'Go on! It's not that hard.'

'No, I . . .' But before I got any further, Semira put the knitting in my hands. I sighed, though I had been told to make her feel at home, hadn't I?

'So, I hold these stick things?'

'They're called needles.'

I shivered because I CAN'T STAND needles. 'And you . . . ?'

'Hook that needle under that hoop of wool.'

'O-kay.'

'And, once you've done that, you hook it under the other one, and then you bring it back over the top of the first one. That's it!'

I managed to do what Semira had told me and she squealed, before clapping her hands together. I felt that I'd done enough and held the knitting out to her, but before she could take it, the door opened.

'Cymbeline!' exclaimed Mrs Robinson. 'Wow! You have been busy during lockdown.'

'What?' I said.

'Learning new skills. What is that?'

I looked down at the knitting in my hand. 'It's . . .'

'Yes?'

'A little hatty.'

'For my mum's new baby,' Semira cut in.

'Cymbeline!' Mrs Robinson exclaimed, again. 'Making a little hatty for Semira's new sibling. How lovely of you! What knitting stitch are you using?'

'Er . . .'

'Cable,' Semira said.

'Then double wow. That's hard. You can show me at breaktime, Cymbeline. But pop it away now and we'll get on, okay?'

I was about to try to explain, but Mrs Robinson wasn't listening. I just sighed, dropped the soon-to-be little hatty on the table behind me, and opened the laptop Mrs Robinson put in front of me.

Then, and to my surprise, Mrs Robinson walked over to the teacher's desk.

'Where's Mr Ashe?' I asked.

Mrs Robinson was reaching over to turn on the whiteboard. 'On a course. Log on, will you?'

And Semira did, while I slumped in my chair. This was yet another disappointment. Not only was Semira the only one there, but we had Mrs Robinson too.

Soon, though, I got a surprise. When I did log on, I thought my misery was complete because the first thing was maths. But Semira put her hand up.

'Miss?' she said. 'Do we have to start with this? I mean, DO we?'

CHAPTER THIRTY

Mrs Robinson stopped what she was doing and peered over the top of her glasses. She seemed confused that Semira was even asking the question. I assumed Semira was in for one of Mrs Robinson's 'Get on with it, please' orders, but before Mrs Robinson could issue it, Semira rushed to explain.

'We want to work on our projects for Mrs Stebbings,' she said.

And, to my immense surprise, Mrs Robinson didn't even tut. Instead, after thinking about it for a second, she said that was a really good idea. Mr Ashe had told her about the plan for the projects and, actually, we should try to get it done as soon as possible. She asked what we were doing.

'Cymbeline?'

'I'm supposed to be drawing something for Mrs Stebbings. I haven't been able to start it, though.'

'And you, Semira?' Mrs Robinson smiled.

'I'm making a map.'

'She's into maps,' I explained.

'It's a map of this area,' Semira went on. 'During World War Two.'

'Is it now?'

Mrs Robinson was clearly into maps too because she came over to the table to have a look. Semira slid a cardboard folder out of her bag and produced a folded-up piece of paper, which she spread out on the table. Mrs Robinson and I squinted at it and I could see what Semira meant. It was two-thirds of a hand-drawn map of Blackheath. The village was there, and the church, with our school marked out in the middle. There were differences, though. Some of the houses across from us weren't on there. The main road looked smaller than I knew it was, and there were things on the heath itself that I didn't recognise.

'What are those?' I said, interested in spite of myself. I pointed to one of the symbols Semira had drawn.

'Searchlights,' she said.

'What?'

'For lighting up enemy bombers,' Semira explained. 'They had them on the heath in the war. Those things there are ack-ack batteries.'

'Ack-ack . . . ?'

'Anti-aircraft guns. Mobile ones. They were to shoot the bombers down. There was lots of bombing near here.'

'Were they trying hit Millwall?'

'Mostly they were aiming at the docks,' Semira said. 'A lot of bombs fell on the heath, though, including right outside here.'

'Excellent work,' said Mrs Robinson, and I actually had to agree. I asked Semira where she got her information from.

'The internet,' Semira explained. 'I read about the searchlights in a blog. Then I looked on old maps.'

'Old . . . ?'

'Maps. I told you I like them. You can find them online too. They show you what places used to look like. Here.'

Semira turned towards her laptop. She went onto Google and soon an old-fashioned-looking map of

London filled the screen. She zoomed it in to Blackheath and I turned from it to the one she'd drawn.

'And this is the one you copied?' Mrs Robinson asked.

Semira nodded, and I sat up, excitement building in my chest. I studied the map, and then reached forward. I put my finger on Semira's mousepad and shifted Semira's zoomed-in portion of Blackheath over to Greenwich. I saw the park. I saw a railway station that I was pretty sure wasn't there now. That was pretty interesting, but I moved away, towards Lewisham. I found Lewisham station, intending to follow the line of the DLR, though it wasn't there then, was it? So I followed the river.

The Ravensbourne River.

And then I stopped, and zoomed in even more, before sticking my index finger right onto the screen.

At Thread Street.

CHAPTER THIRTY-ONE

'Yes!' I exclaimed.

It was there!

Thread Street was right where Mr Stebbings had said it would be: just on from the allotments, which were clearly marked. I was excited. Google Maps was clearly wrong, but how had Mum and I missed it when we'd gone looking? I didn't know, but we could go down later! I couldn't hide my excitement and Mrs Robinson asked why I was 'getting in such a tizzy'. I told her how I'd wanted to draw the Stebbings's street. She said that was a lovely idea, but I probably wouldn't have time. Not if I hadn't actually begun. Everyone else's projects were well under way.

'But you've time now, so why not draw a general wartime scene?' she said. She even found me one online of a street party. She told me to copy it and I did – but it wasn't the same! I wanted to draw the Stebbings's *actual* street! I'd put a football in it. I'd draw a broken window. I'd draw a little girl peeking out from behind a van, and I'd draw a little boy getting 'what for'. The picture would be unique, and I was CERTAIN that Mrs Stebbings would LOVE it, though that made me think of the other thing she'd love.

My shirt.

Again, I thought about how I'd overslept last night and I sighed, calling myself an idiot until the bell went.

Semira didn't seem to notice the bell. She just went on adding things to her map. That made me feel even more useless, and I stood up and trudged downstairs into the playground. The empty playground. Without anyone on the snakes and ladders or up on the platform at the end, it looked wrong – sort of pointless, though not as bad as the thing I saw when I looked behind me.

I'd emerged next to the big windows and I peered through them into the hall. It was empty too. The piano looked dusty and a piece of paper was lying underneath the noticeboard. It must have fallen off. I turned from it to the blue plastic lunch seats, folded away against the wall bars. Then I pictured them out, and full, with Mrs Stebbings in the middle of them like the conductor of an unruly orchestra. The image was so real, but would it ever become a reality? Would Mrs Stebbings's voice ever ring round that hall again? The thought that it might not brought a lump to my throat, and I clenched my fists, hot tears at the back of my eyes – as I realised something.

I wasn't a nurse. I wasn't a doctor. I couldn't save Mrs Stebbings. But there WAS something I could do. It wasn't big, but Mr Stebbings had said it would help – so I'd do it, and I wouldn't wait any longer to do it either. I SHOULD have gone to get my shirt back last night! There was no point dwelling on that, though.

I had to act. I had to get the shirt back!

And I had to do it now.

I'd never sneaked out of school before. I'd never done anything LIKE sneaking out of school. I turned round, feeling determined as I marched across the playground, past the big chessboard and then alongside the mural of kids from the past. I saw the office. All

I had to do was get past it without being noticed. Then I'd hit the green button, wait a second, and run. Though . . .

What were *they* doing there?

No wonder the playground was empty. All of Key Stage One were lining up at the front of the school with their bags. I frowned at them, and then frowned at Mrs Robinson and Semira, who were coming out of the main door. Mrs Robinson had my bag and coat with her.

'There you are,' she said. 'I'm not your packhorse, you know!' Mrs Robinson held my bag and coat out and – confused – I took them. She laughed. 'Didn't your mum tell you?'

'Tell me?' I said.

'She can't have read her email properly. Never mind. You've got a packed lunch, I take it?'

'Yes,' I said. 'But where are we going?'

'Where . . . ? Heavens, boy. How long have you been at this school? It's the first Thursday of the month.'

'The . . . ?'

'Allotment day! Just DON'T push me into the pond this time, okay?'

CHAPTER THIRTY-TWO

Five minutes later we were walking across the heath. Semira and I were out in front to keep the bubbles apart. Mrs Robinson was telling us how we had to stay distanced from Key Stage One when we got there, but I wasn't paying much attention. I was trying to work out how I'd get from the allotments to Mulberry Park. They were right next to each other, but it seemed even harder to pull off than my plan to escape school. Mrs Robinson would be right there. She'd be keeping her beady eyes on us. When Mrs Robinson hung back a bit to talk to Miss Phillips, I hissed out a sigh.

'What's the matter?' Semira asked.

'It's nothing.'

'You sure?'

I just shook my head and Semira bit her lip. 'I'm sorry,' she said.

I frowned. 'What about?'

'Mrs Stebbings. I only met her once, but she was lovely. My first day. There was this incredible pudding. She asked if I was new. Oh!'

'What?'

'She asked if I supported Charlton too. She was really nice to me.'

'She's nice to everyone,' I said.

'And that's why you want to do that special picture?'

I took another deep breath. 'Yes.'

'Will this help, then?'

Semira reached into her bag, though not for knitting this time. She pulled out a folded-up piece of paper, which I took from her – and I stared at it. It was the portion of the old map that I'd been looking at online.

'I printed it out for you,' Semira explained.

'Thanks!' I said, and I meant it – though it still didn't solve the problem of how I would get to Mulberry Park. How could I get my shirt back?

I was still squeezing my brain round it when we actually reached the allotments. I stared at the bridge leading over the DLR track. I was SO close! The tent was just metres away! I could almost see it. Mrs Robinson asked me to help her get all the tools out, though, so I turned away and got on with it.

First, I had to spray the tools with sanitiser. Then I had to lay them out for the Key Stage One kids, who were waiting just inside the gates with Miss Phillips and Mr Amritraj. They'd all brought wellies, though Semira and I had to use spare ones. I put mine on, my eyes flicking towards the park again. Over the wall I could make out the top of a tree and I realised that it was the big one in the clearing! It was SO CLOSE. I stamped my feet in frustration.

'Cymbeline?' Mrs Robinson said.

She was lifting a big bag of compost out of the shed with both hands. Once she'd set it down, she walked over to me, a mixture of concern, curiosity and irritation on her face. And I thought about it. I wanted to just tell her – like I'd wanted to tell Mum: a girl living in Mulberry Park had the shirt I needed for our video! But Mrs Robinson would tell on the girl. She was a teacher, which meant that she'd have to. But should I do it anyway?

Mrs Robinson was squinting at me and I didn't know what to do – until Semira said, 'It's his picture.'

Mrs Robinson turned to her. 'What about it, Semira? I thought he did it this morning.'

'Yes, but he wants it to be of the *actual* street,' Semira explained.

Mrs Robinson dusted some compost off her hands. 'I know, but . . .'

'Couldn't we just go and find it? Not for him, of course. For Mrs Stebbings! Couldn't we, miss?'

Semira was looking up at Mrs Robinson, her face plastered with hope. I didn't share it. What Semira didn't quite appreciate was that this was Mrs Robinson! She may have let us do our projects early, but that was a fluke. She was well tough, and she knew every trick in the book.

When we had her in Year Three, Lance told her that he hadn't done his 'My Maths' the night before because his internet had been down. But Mrs Robinson called BT, who told her that there had been a perfect service all week – BUSTED!

The next day we had the Weekly Mile, where we had to jog round the heath. Billy claimed that his leg was hurting (it SO wasn't) and I expected Mrs Robinson to tell him to do it anyway. But she didn't. Instead, Mrs Robinson said okay, he could sit it out.

Billy beamed, and did a 'Loser!' sign at me when Mrs Robinson wasn't looking. But guess what? She didn't make us do the Weekly Mile at all. She said she'd changed her mind and that we could have a football match instead! And she wouldn't let Billy play! She even told Mr Ashe that Billy shouldn't go to Saturday football at the weekend, because of his injured leg.

So Semira had no chance, did she? Mrs Robinson would shake her head and tell us to 'GET. ON.'

Except . . .

She didn't.

Semira was looking up at Mrs Robinson with this very still, calm smile on her face – and the weirdest thing happened. Mrs Robinson started to dismiss her, but then began to soften. And then, without any drama at all, Mrs Robinson just . . . agreed! She did! And I gawped at Semira, ever so slightly scared because she was clearly in possession of some sort of superpower. She could control Mrs Robinson WITH HER MIND, which made me realise something.

I'd finally seen one in action. Semira was that legendary thing, which I'd never really believed ACTUALLY existed.

A Teacher Whisperer.

I was stunned. Not sure how long it would last, though, I snapped into action. I pulled the map Semira had printed out from my pocket. I then strode through the allotment gates, leading Semira and Mrs Robinson towards the troll bridge. I led them over it into the park. I hurried along the path and, when we got to the little playground (no Millwall baby) Mrs Robinson asked for the map. I handed it to her. She pushed her glasses on top of her head and studied it, looking confused until a DLR train came grinding by on its way into Elverson Road.

Then she nodded.

'Of course,' she said.

I frowned at her. 'Of course?'

'Well, that explains it. Don't you see?'

'See what?'

'Look, Cymbeline. Look at Thread Street,' Mrs Robinson said.

Mrs Robinson held the map out to me then, and I did look at it. And I realised: Mum and I weren't wrong. Thread Street WAS right there: where the DLR track was now, on the other side of the river. The whole street must have been knocked down – to make the track and the station!

How stupid I'd been. When I'd seen Mr Stebbings at Lewisham Hospital, he must have known that Thread Street wasn't there any more – but I hadn't asked him. And he didn't know that I wanted to *go* there. I was so disappointed, but I told myself not to worry. The street wasn't the main thing, was it?

I had to get the shirt.

And I was SO close.

So I turned to Mrs Robinson.

'It *was* there,' I said. 'You can see it on the map.'

'That's right.'

'So maybe there's still a trace of it.'

'Of Thread Street? I shouldn't . . .'

'Some bricks,' I insisted. 'Or a wall or two.'

'You never know. But . . .'

'Great. I won't be long.'

Mrs Robinson blinked at me. 'Long?'

'Don't worry,' I said. 'I've got wellies on.'

And, before Mrs Robinson could say anything else, I ran.

It wasn't easy because the wellies were too big, but I got over the little wall fast enough. I slapped my way down the bank and splashed into the water. I grabbed the long branch and pulled myself towards the far side. I got over the squelchy bit and scrambled up towards the green tunnel. I crawled through it and – YES! – I emerged into the clearing.

Not that I was looking for any sign of Thread Street. I took in the metal box I'd seen before. Beyond it was the big, spreading tree. I was about to rush past it, but I stumbled, and stopped, before my hands went to my hips.

And I stared.

At nothing.

Nothing at all.

Because the sagging old tent was **GONE.**

CHAPTER THIRTY-THREE

Have you ever had that feeling, like everything inside you is just draining right out?

And there's nothing you can do about it?

I had it then as I realised something. I'd been SO scared when I'd been there before – scared of the place, and of the fox. I hadn't been half as scared as the girl must have been, though. She'd have been terrified that I'd tell on her. She'd begged me not to in her note, but she didn't know me, did she? So she wouldn't have known whether or not I'd do it anyway. I hadn't found a way to reassure her.

So she'd gone.

She'd found somewhere else to live.

But would it be safe? Or would someone else find her?

And there was another problem.

This meant that I'd lost my shirt – the shirt I needed to give Mrs Stebbings – for ever.

Except . . .

'Who are you?' a voice said.

I froze. Then I spun round – and a girl was standing there. A different girl. She was holding the spade that had been propped up against the tree the last time I was here. She was older than the first girl – about sixteen or seventeen. Her hair was dark too, but longer, framing her face like a doorway. Her eyes were the same though: almost black and SO fierce.

I swallowed. 'I'm . . .'

'Wait.' The girl stepped forward, the spade still in her hand. 'You're *him*,' she hissed. 'Aren't you?'

'Er, which him exactly?'

'Cymbeline. Wansa told me. You're the one who came here to spy on us. You're the one who tried to catch her with the raspberries.'

'No!' I exclaimed. 'I didn't. I just came here for . . .'

'What?'

I sighed. Then I swallowed as the girl's dark eyes bored into me. 'My mum left some things outside our house,' I garbled. 'For people to take. Only, she put my football shirt out by mistake. It's special. I need it. I really need it. Is Wansa the other girl I saw here?'

The girl nodded.

'And you are . . . ?'

The girl tilted her chin up and didn't answer, but I knew. They were sisters. So, 'us' in the girl's note referred to her, not the fox.

'Where's your tent?' I said.

The girl glowered at me, but she pointed towards some bushes on the other side of the clearing. There was a bin bag there.

'I see,' I said. 'So . . . ?'

'What?'

'You haven't actually gone, then?'

The girl sighed. 'No. I'm guarding our stuff. In case someone like you comes along. Wansa is looking for somewhere else.'

'Why?' I asked.

'Because you ruined it. By coming here. This place . . .' Her eyes flicked round the clearing.

'Yes?'

'It's perfect.'

What? An old tent in a scruffy bit of wood? There was no kitchen. No bathroom. No washing machine. What did they keep their food in? And if it got really cold . . . I couldn't understand it. 'Then why leave?'

'Because of you. We didn't know if we could trust you.'

'But you can!' I insisted. 'I don't care that you're here. I won't tell, I promise.'

'How can we know that?'

'Well, I haven't told so far, have I?'

'Well, what about her?' the girl said, and for a second I had no idea what she was talking about. But, when I turned to look over my shoulder, I saw Semira – crawling out of the green tunnel.

'I didn't tell her,' I insisted. 'I promise. She must have followed me. She's in my class.'

'I'm his friend,' Semira said.

'Yes. And she won't tell anyone.'

'How can I possibly know that?' the girl said, and I tried to reply. But what could I say? Maybe Semira *would* tell. Maybe she'd turn right round and run off to Mrs Robinson. The girl must have been thinking something similar because, when I didn't answer, her body changed position. She leaned away from us and began to move, shooting a glance at the far end of the clearing where there must have been another way out. She was going to run. I knew it. Then she'd be gone.

I was about to stammer something, anything, when Semira said, 'I won't tell.'

Semira's voice was firm, but it didn't stop the girl. She started to edge back further, about to spring away when Semira added, 'Because I know you.'

That did stop the girl.

'You . . . ?'

'And your sister. Not personally. But I know why you're hiding here.'

'How?' The girl's chin jutted up again. She was halfway between running and staying.

'Because I've walked in your shoes,' Semira said.

CHAPTER THIRTY-FOUR

There was silence.

Well, not *silence*-silence because we were in London. There was car noise, and DLR noise, and bird noise, and people in the park noise – but there was silence in that clearing. I wanted to break it – because . . . what was Semira on about? I bit my lip though. I had a strange sense that Semira should do the talking and that, for once, I, Cymbeline Igloo, should say absolutely NOTHING.

'What do you mean?' the girl said.

Semira lowered her head. 'I was not born in this country,' she stated.

The girl took that in. 'No?'

'No. I'm a refugee.'

The word seemed to sit in the space between us, the girl studying it like a painting. 'From where?' she demanded.

'Eritrea,' Semira said. 'Have you heard of it?'

The girl shook her head. I'm ashamed to say that I did, too.

'It's in East Africa. It's very beautiful. There are mountains and incredible birds, all sorts of animals like elephants and leopards and . . .'

'So why did you leave?' the girl said, her eyes fixed on Semira's.

Semira lowered her head. 'There was a war there. When I was younger.'

'There was a war in my country too,' the girl said. 'Were there bombs?'

Semira nodded. Her hands clasped, then unclasped. 'Mostly, they dropped them in the night. My dad used to comfort us. But . . .'

'Yes?' the girl said.

'He was a doctor so he wasn't supposed to fight. But he got taken away. Into the army. He . . .' Semira took a big breath. 'Didn't come back.' I turned to Semira and gasped, though she kept her eyes on the girl. 'Then my mum heard that they were coming to take my brothers too, even though they were too young. So . . .'

'So?'

'She led us away.'

'To here?'

'No, Cymbeline.' Semira grimaced. 'First, we went into the forest.'

'With your brothers?'

'Yes. We were very hungry but we thought we could wait until the war ended. Live there. But the soldiers came. We only just escaped. Our uncle helped us. We got over the border, into Ethiopia. From there, we went to many different places. Many different countries. We stayed in refugee camps. My mum knew English and she taught us. One day, I'll tell you, but eventually, yes, we came here. Is . . .'

'Yes?' the girl asked.

'Is that what happened to you?'

The question stopped the girl in her tracks. She grimaced again, and a muscle in her face twitched. Her gaze moved away from Semira but not to anything physical. It was as if she'd gone somewhere, was seeing other things. I swallowed, wondering what those things were, though I was also afraid of finding out. After a while, the pictures seemed to fade in the girl's eyes, and she swallowed.

'It was like that, only . . .'

'Yes?' Semira's voice was soft, like a handkerchief.

'I have no brothers. So it was me the soldiers took. Daesh, we called them. In my country. Syria.'

'What happened?' I said. 'I mean, did you escape too?'

'Eventually. I got away. Then me and Wansa . . .'

'Your sister?'

The girl nodded. 'We walked. We walked and walked. So much that . . .'

'Yes?'

'Our shoes broke. Wansa kept me going.'

'But isn't she younger than you?'

The girl turned to me. 'Under Daesh, it is easier for a girl to be younger. Now she says we can't stay here. She says they'll separate us. She says they'll send us back.'

'But we won't tell!' I insisted, and I could see that the girl wanted to believe me. Was that because this place was, unbelievably, so much better than all the other places she'd had to live? I didn't know, but I suddenly realised how tired she looked. She was leaning against the spade, and I blinked at it.

Without knowing why, really, I asked, 'What is that for, anyway?'

The girl looked caught out. She blushed, embarrassed and angry for some reason – so I quickly changed the subject.

'Wait, never mind that. Please don't let Wansa take you away. Stay here, where you like it. Or at least keep your sister here,' I pleaded, 'until I can speak to her. Please! Just—'

'Cymbeline! Semira! Come ALONG now, please.'

The voice seemed to cut into the clearing like a knife. It was Mrs Robinson's of course. She was calling from the park.

Semira looked nervous. She turned to the green tunnel, while I kept looking at the girl.

'What's your name?' I asked.

The girl blinked at me and the tiniest of smiles formed on her lips.

'Meyan,' she whispered, and I wanted to reply. I wanted to beg her once more to get her sister to stay.

But Mrs Robinson called out for me again.

CHAPTER THIRTY-FIVE

It was strange to be back in Mulberry Park.

The normal world.

Crossing the river had been like slipping through a portal into two other people's lives. I glanced at Semira, almost unable to believe the things she'd told me. She was only my age – she might even have been a bit younger – but so much had happened to her.

Even more seemed to have happened to Meyan and Wansa, but were they right to be so scared of being found? Would they really be split up? Or sent away? I couldn't believe our government would ever do such a thing, until I remembered something else I'd seen on the news with Mum. Not about coronavirus. There were these boats, which had sailed over from France. Some politicians wanted to send them back. Even when they were allowed to stay, the people onboard were kept in these horrible detention centres. But what if they all had stories to tell like the ones that I'd just heard? What had they possibly done to deserve that?

Something else was bothering me too: the spade. I'd wondered what it was for, but now I wondered why Meyan had been so odd about it.

I couldn't work it out, but, once we were back at the allotments, I used a different spade to dig some shallow trenches. The Key Stage One kids came after I'd finished and sprinkled seeds in. They all seemed so excited and I wanted to join in their happiness, but I couldn't keep my mind away from Wansa.

Would she agree to wait for me, and give me back my shirt? If she did, how could I possibly get to her without my mum knowing? Could I bring Mum to Mulberry Park later, and leave her sketching while I went off? No. She'd never let me go out again today. The only thing I could think of was to wait for night-time again, and this time stay awake – though would that fox be standing guard?

*

As we walked back to school, I kept thinking about Wansa and Meyan. When we got there though, I had to put my worries aside – and do the maths we'd avoided before. Then Mrs Robinson let us do our projects again. I worked on my picture. I changed the sign in the photograph to Thread Street, while Semira extended her map. We had another video call then, which I didn't think would be the same with Mrs Robinson instead of Mr Ashe. It was great, though. This was because of what everyone had done on their projects. Mrs Robinson asked Veronique to go first and she picked up her ukulele (she can play anything). She sang the 'We'll Meet Again' song that Mr Ashe had mentioned, and it was great.

'We all have to sing it,' Vi said, when Veronique had finished. 'Meanwhile, can I show you my project?'

Mrs Robinson said yes, and Vi shared her screen with us. She'd done this amazing PowerPoint about rationing. It must have taken her hours. Meanwhile, Daisy had made a cake with her dad, using only World War Two ingredients.

'I had to do with margarine instead of butter, and no eggs.'

'What's it like?' I asked, and Daisy grimaced.

'It's not exactly the STP,' she said.

I laughed, but then I just stared: because what Lance had done on Charlton was QUALITY. He'd made a PowerPoint too. There were dates and tables and loads of photos – including one of the bomber-spotters at the Valley that he'd mentioned. There was also one of Charlton station, where we get off when we go to home games. A rocket had totally destroyed it, killing the wife of the stationmaster.

'And this is her name on the plaque outside the ground,' Lance said. 'She probably went to the matches. Next time I go, I'm going to shout extra loud, just for her.'

I nodded, certain that Mrs Stebbings would think that all of this was AMAZING – if we could only get it to her. Mrs Robinson seemed to be having the same thought. She told everyone to send in pictures and videos later that day. She'd put them all together.

'And you'll introduce it, Cymbeline,' she said. 'Since it was your idea, I believe.'

'I'll record it tomorrow,' I said. 'At ten o'clock in the morning. I'll go and do it outside the Stebbings's house.'

'She'll like that,' Mrs Robinson said.

'Yes.' I took a breath. Then, very loudly, and very slowly, I said, 'So that's where I'll be. TOMORROW. AT TEN O'CLOCK IN THE MORNING. OUTSIDE THE STEBBINGS'S HOUSE, WHICH IS ON MORPETH HILL, JUST OFF THE MAIN ROAD TO LEWISHAM FROM GREENWICH.

OKAY?'

Loads of yellow thumbs went up, and then the video call was over.

Semira and I had an hour of school left, so we went back to our projects. I did add a little girl to my street scene, plus a football and a broken window. When I saw Semira push her map to the side, I asked if it was finished.

'Not quite.'

'You've covered a whole page, though.'

'I know. But now I've got to add the bombs.'

'What?'

'The ones that fell.'

'But how will you know where to put them? I mean, other than on Charlton station?'

'Because of this,' Semira said. She showed me another map – and this one was absolutely amazing.

It was on the internet again. Semira turned her laptop so that I could see, and typed in 'www.bombsight.org'. What appeared was a map of London, pretty much like a normal one except for one thing: every single bomb that had fallen on London in World War Two was shown there.

Each one was marked with a little red bomb symbol, which you could click on. When you did, it told you what kind of bomb had landed. I chose one at random and a box came up to tell me that it was a 'High Explosive Bomb'. Another one was a 'Parachute Bomb', which I'd never heard of. I found Charlton station and discovered that a 'V2 rocket' had destroyed it, something I wanted to tell Lance. In one case there was a record of a bomb falling but no record of it going off.

'Move over to Blackheath,' I said.

Semira did – and SO MANY bombs had hit it! Two had even landed right outside our school.

'What are "Incendiary Bombs"?' I asked, squinting at the screen.

Mrs Robinson had come over to our table. She shivered. 'Fire bombs,' she said. 'Filled with oil. They were dropped to make things burn. Just imagine.'

I shivered too, and then spotted something: a link titled 'Nearby Images'. I clicked on that and saw a photo of a school in Woolwich, which isn't far from Blackheath. It must have been bombed, because the windows were all blown out and there was a big pile of rubble in the playground – but kids were still there. They were having playtime. I shook my head. This Home Front subject was not so boring after all.

After we'd looked at the photo for a few seconds, Mrs Robinson clicked on another. This one showed the same school, but now the kids were wearing massive gasmasks that made them look like baby elephants. They made the little facemasks that people were having to wear now to protect against coronavirus look like nothing.

'Children had to carry them everywhere,' Mrs Robinson said. 'But that wasn't the worse thing for them.'

'Was that the food?' I said.

'No.'

'Or the fear of being bombed?' said Semira.

'Well, these photos were taken early in the war. Most of these children would have been evacuated soon after this. They'd have gone to live in the countryside, which was less likely to be bombed.'

'So what was the worst thing?' I asked.

'Knowing that their dads and older brothers were off fighting. Every day they would have wondered if they'd ever see them again. Think about that, Cymbeline.'

I did. And I wish Mrs Robinson hadn't mentioned it because Semira was thinking about it too. How could she not be, when the very same thing had happened to her? Mrs Robinson can't have known Semira's story. I gave Semira the most sympathetic look I could, and then turned back to the photograph. Some of the kids in it were younger than me, yet they'd had to deal with so much terrible stuff. I thought of my own dad. I don't see him that much, but what would it be like knowing he was away, fighting in a war? I could really imagine it now, which was probably because of what Semira and Meyan had told me in Mulberry Park. It made me go quiet inside – and think of myself. I got so bound up in my own problems. They always seemed so massive to me, but were they really?

The answer to that was no. They weren't big at all – something that I saw even more clearly after Mum had come to take me home.

Because the biggest problem that I had in the WHOLE of my life was about to be solved.

CHAPTER THIRTY-SIX

Mum picked me up ten minutes after school finished. Once we were in the car, I asked how work had been for her. She said fine – it was all really clean and safe.

'And the head gave me a little present,' she said. 'For helping.'

'Ooh, what?'

'She'd managed to get a big sack of flour delivered from a catering company. Everyone got a bit.'

'So . . . ?'

'Pancakes!' Mum said. 'I'll make some after tea.'

I said that would be epic, and then Mum asked how *my* day had been. I said it had been good, actually. I told her about Semira's maps and how we'd gone to the allotments. I didn't tell her about going across the river, but I did tell her about Thread Street.

'Of course!' Mum said. 'Well, what a shame. But you're doing another picture?'

I said I was. 'I'd still like to go to Mulberry Park, though. I can do a drawing of what Thread Street looks like now.'

But, just as I'd feared, Mum said *not today* – and she was firm. She parked the car and we got out. I followed her across the road towards our front door, which she unlocked.

And then she screamed.

'Cym!' she cried. 'Look!'

And there, lying on the hall floor, underneath the letterbox, was a puddle of shiny red material.

My Charlton shirt!

I was hardly able to move.

But then I pushed Mum aside. I grabbed the shirt and stared at it – and yes! It was the right one! I pressed it to my face. Then I ran into the kitchen, first making sure the table was clean before spreading the shirt out. The signatures were there. I scrutinised each one – even Brett Casey's – but the shirt seemed to have suffered no damage.

'Put it on,' Mum squealed, and I did, Mum shaking her head in disbelief.

'But how . . . ?' she said.

'How? Well . . .'

'Well?'

I blinked at her. 'The person who took it must have brought it back.'

'Obviously!' Mum laughed. 'But why?'

'Er . . .' I couldn't tell her that Meyan must have told Wansa how much I needed it. 'Whoever it was must have seen the signatures. They must have realised that it was special and that you didn't mean to give it away.'

'I suppose,' Mum said. 'Or . . .'

'What?'

She laughed. 'They just grabbed it with the other stuff – and they were Millwall fans!'

'Not funny,' I said, not able to contemplate the idea of my shirt being in the hands of the enemy, even if I did know it wasn't true. 'And it can't have been that.'

'Why not?'

'They would have cut it up with scissors. But who cares? **I'VE GOT MY SHIRT BACK!**'

And happiness thudded through me like water out of the bath tap.

I took the shirt off and checked again for damage. There really wasn't any and I was so relieved. It felt like one of the best things that had ever happened to me – until I realised something. Mum promised that we'd keep the shirt safe. She'd lock it up until she could get it framed again. But, while she was folding it up, I started to feel a bit squelchy in my stomach. And it was guilt – because my joy at finding my shirt was all about ME. I was really supposed to be happy because of Mrs Stebbings, because I could wear the shirt in the video and then give it to her.

And I realised something else. It was SO cool of Wansa to bring my shirt back. I pictured her seeing the clothes outside our house. For her and Meyan, it must have been like finding a hoard of treasure. Wansa didn't see the shirt as an amazing thing to hang on a wall, did she? No. She saw it as something to wear. To keep her warm. Yet she'd given it back to me.

And what had I given her?

The answer to that was nothing.

Nothing AT ALL.

Which was something I was going to put right.

I told Mum I was going upstairs to change out of my school uniform. I did that, but I also stuffed an old backpack with clothes. Back downstairs, I told Mum that she'd missed Bobby Bunns again. While she was jumping up and down in the living room, I went into the food cupboard. Mum had bought a big bag of rice at the supermarket and I emptied some out into a plastic bag. She'd got some tins of spaghetti hoops too, and I took three. I found a pack of biscuits and some hot chocolate powder – and then I looked in the fridge. From there I took a pat of butter, a bottle of milk, and the only vegetable that was sitting at the bottom.

A cauliflower.

Well, they might like it, mightn't they?

I knew Mum might notice the missing food but, if she did, I'd deal with it then. I stashed the backpack in the scarves and hats basket, which is near the front door. I got my torch and shoved it in too, though I knew I might not need it. I saw a chance to get to the park while it was still light: during Clap for Carers.

I *thought* I might be able to slip away, while Mum was busy on the street banging pots and pans together. I soon realised that I couldn't, though – not only did she stay close to our door but she would have noticed the backpack anyway. That was frustrating, and more so when Mum really got into the clapping, probably because she was so happy about my shirt. She had two pans, like normal, but she banged them together so hard that one of the handles snapped. The pan spun into the road – and got run over by a car!

I thought was pretty funny at first, until Mum said, 'Sorry, Cym.' She picked the pan up from the road. It was wrecked, though I didn't know why Mum was apologising to me – until I saw which pan it was.

The frying pan.

'Which means . . . ?'

'No pancakes,' Mum winced.

I didn't make a fuss. After Clap for Carers, I did the last bits on my picture, and then Mum helped start on the Anderson shelter (model version). Soon it was time for bed, though, and this time Mum wasn't far behind me.

I don't know if she was asleep, but she wouldn't have heard me anyway. I was ninja-quiet. I slid out of bed and picked my way downstairs. I slipped my trainers on, picked up my backpack and unlocked the front door.

Outside, it was quiet, and not that dark because of the streetlights. I hurried towards the DLR station, stopping in my tracks when a fox skipped out into the road from behind a parked car. It was only a small one, though, and it ignored me. I nodded: if it was time for foxes to be out and about, then maybe THE fox would be gone from the clearing. I pushed on, turning right towards the troll bridge. I breathed a sigh of relief to see that it was empty but I still stopped halfway along.

Because of the trees.

The trees in Mulberry Park looked massive, as if they'd turned black and grown twice as high since sunset. They loomed over me as I walked on along the path; some laughter from behind made me jump. It didn't stop me though. By the end of the little wall, I reached into my backpack for my torch. At the edge of the river, I took my trainers off and waded into the water. Halfway across I stopped: there was a harsh scraping noise. I moved on, pushed through the green tunnel as quietly as I could, and immediately saw what was making the sound.

I'd expected the clearing to be in darkness, which it was. It wasn't pitch black though: strips of orange light were cutting through it from the DLR track. In one, I could see Wansa. She was on the very left of the clearing, near to where the bushes got really thick. I nearly called out to her – but she was digging. Her spade struck something hard and she hissed, before moving to her right and trying again – while I frowned.

I don't like unsolved mysteries, no matter how small they are. I like knowing what's going on. So, once I'd given her the food, and the clothes, and thanked her for my shirt, I'd ask her what she was doing.

Except . . .

Suddenly, and very certainly, I knew.

And the knowledge made me feel terrible. It made me feel worse than I had before, though it wasn't guilt I felt now. It was shame.

Meyan hadn't looked embarrassed and angry when I'd asked her about the spade. She'd looked humiliated, and Wansa would feel that too, if she saw me there.

I decided to leave the bag of stuff. They'd find it in the morning, wouldn't they? I did that and backed out, as quietly as I could, before stepping back over the river. I put my trainers on and ran all the way home, sneaking back in and then up to bed, where I pulled my duvet tight round me.

And I thought of them in their sagging tent, how

they didn't have proper beds. Or a kitchen. Or a bathroom. Well, I knew now that there was something else they didn't have.

A toilet.

It wasn't fair. They shouldn't have to live like that, just as people shouldn't have bombs dropped on them, not eighty years ago or today. Never. I took some deep breaths and shook my head because I had to DO something for them. I had no idea what I COULD do, though, because they didn't want anyone to know that they were there.

It was SO frustrating – until next morning, when I did find out what I could do.

Though not before Mum had turned my WHOLE WORLD upside d

o

w

n.

CHAPTER THIRTY-SEVEN

I found her downstairs.

She was at the kitchen table again, with her phone propped up against the Weetabix like it had been so many times recently. It was off, though, so she wasn't looking at it. Instead, she was staring into space, a thousand thoughts seeming to flit across her face. When she saw me, she took a second before giving me a closed-mouthed smile. Then she pulled me onto her lap.

'Hello, you,' she said.

'Hello, you.'

Mum pushed my hair back behind my ear, and then looked at me – like she was trying to find the meaning to something on my face. Her face was very still, and serious. I took a breath and glanced again at her phone.

'Can you tell me?' I said.

Mum bit her lip. 'About what, love?'

'Mum.' I sighed. 'You know what. About . . .'

'Yes?'

'You and Stephan. I know there's something going on. I can tell. Are you . . . ?'

Mum took a big breath and let it out slowly. 'What, Cym?'

I swallowed. 'Going to break up? Doesn't he want to marry you any more?'

Mum didn't answer for a second, and I bit my lip. As I said before, at first I wasn't sure about Stephan. But now I liked him. I really liked him. He was kind. He was positive, always trying to do things, and Ellen and Mabel were part of my life now. I'd got used to it all. That had made all the difference, and I was really happy about the future. Our future. I'd even planned out what we were going to do when they got back. Stephan still hadn't been to the Valley to see Charlton. I was going to take him when it opened again (without Mum, who wouldn't let us get battered sausages from the fish and chip shop). I was going to take Mabel and Ellen to the Tate Modern in central London, though not to look at the pictures. There's this big slope inside that you can chase pound coins down. It's epic. Afterwards we'd go to these fountains nearby that turn on and off and get you wet when you run through them.

And then?

Then we'd just live. We'd be together, the best thing being that Mum would be happy. I said how she gets depressed sometimes. I knew she'd have to go on dealing with that, but being with Stephan would help, because she loved him. And he loved her. I KNEW it.

Or, at least, I thought I did.

'Well?' I said, looking into Mum's eyes.

Oddly, she smiled. A proper smile, not a fake one. And she pretended to be a bit . . . cross.

'How could you?' she said.

'How . . . could I? What?'

'Cymbeline Igloo. How could you suggest that someone would not want to marry me?'

I stared. 'So, he still does want to marry you?'

'Of course. Stephan wants to marry me more than ever. Being apart can do that.'

'Then . . . what's the problem?'

'Well . . .' Mum stopped speaking – and she looked serious again.

That made me shake my head because, if they were still getting married, what did she look so worried about? 'Well, WHAT?' I said.

'Well, it's just that we can't decide where.'

'Where what?'

'Where to get married.'

I laughed. 'Does it matter?'

'Yes,' Mum said. 'Because Stephan wants us to get married in New Zealand.'

'What? In New Zealand? Really? That's brilliant!' I exclaimed, picturing the beach I'd seen Mabel on. It looked BRILLIANT. 'Would we go in the summer holidays?'

'We could. But it wouldn't actually matter when. We could go anytime.'

'Anytime? How?'

'Because, Cym, Stephan wants us all to go and live there.'

CHAPTER THIRTY-EIGHT

I stared.

Mouth open.

I could feel my lips, trying to form words, which they couldn't do until I'd got control of them.

'But why?' I said.

'I asked the same question, but it's obvious, isn't it?'

'Obvious?'

Mum sighed. 'You saw, Cym. What it's like there. The space. The beach.'

'But are they really not having a lockdown?'

'No. Not now. They have to take some measures. Everyone's being cautious. But their government has handled it properly. It's maybe easier for them because they're far away, but they've done really well. You can see what Mabel and Ellen are doing. Stephan wants that for us.'

'But it's great here!'

'Is it? Not going out? Being frightened all the time?'

'It won't last forever.'

'I know. But it's going to be a long time before we're back to normal. And . . .'

'What?'

'Being back home with the girls has shown Stephan how lovely it is there – not just during the pandemic but in normal times too. For families.'

'And what have you said to him?'

'Nothing. I promise. It can't happen for a while anyway. We'd have to get special permission to go there. Short-term travel isn't allowed.'

'And you'd have to get on a plane, wouldn't you – with *other people*?'

'I know. But I'd just have to deal with it.'

'But would they even let us go there?'

'Well, Stephan thinks they'd probably make an exception if we were getting married, and going there to live. But all I said is that I'll think about it. That's all.'

'Good. Then you can say no. Can't you? Can't you, Mum?' I insisted, but Mum didn't answer. She just swallowed, and looked away. Then she moved me off her lap and went to take the milk out of the fridge.

I watched her – and stared round the kitchen. It was great. As was our garden. Everything about our house was perfect, and I knew something for certain: so many people would have given everything to have our lives – right here! And not just our family life.

'What about my friends?' I said, and Mum turned round to me.

'You'd make new ones. You know you would. And there's FaceTime, and Zoom, isn't there? You'd still see Lance and Veronique that way.'

'But it's not the same,' I said. 'It's nothing like the same. It's not real life!'

And, at ten o'clock, I realised how right I was.

I normally have two Weetabix, but I barely managed half of one that morning, the other fading down into the milk. I went upstairs and got dressed. When I came downstairs again, Mum had opened the laptop and was looking on the online classroom. She seemed wary of me, but I wasn't going to give her a fight. I had something more important to do, and I'd told everyone where and when I'd be doing it. I just sat down and she told me that Mr Ashe wanted us to work on our projects for the morning.

'Later,' I said. 'I want to finish that English comprehension.'

'Really? You don't want to do any more on that picture for Mrs Stebbings, then?'

'No. All I have to do is make the introduction video.'

'Shall we do that now, then?'

I said no, I wanted to do half an hour of English. Mum shrugged and I got on with it, though at 9.45 I stopped.

'Okay,' I said. 'We can do the video now.'

'Great.' Mum reached for her phone but I stopped her. 'I need to put my shirt on.'

'Okay.'

'And we have to do it outside the Stebbings's house. Mrs Robinson said so.'

'Oh,' Mum said. 'That's okay. Go and get your shoes on, then.'

And I did.

And my shirt.

Then we left, going up past my old nursery and

across the main road. We climbed Morpeth Hill and Mum rang the Stebbings's doorbell, though I knew Mr Stebbings wouldn't be there.

I knew where he'd be.

'Have you heard anything?' I asked. 'From the hospital?' Mum shook her head. 'Which means she's still in Intensive Care?'

'That's right. Shall we start the video?'

'In a second.'

I took Mum's wrist and looked at her watch. It was nearly ten, so I turned towards the top of the hill. There was nothing to see but a couple of cats, and a squirrel on top of a fence.

Until Lance walked round the corner.

Lance was with his dad. Mum turned to me, suspicion crinkling her face up, just as it was crinkling Lance's dad's. And then Mum's mouth opened.

Because Vi and Daisy had appeared at the top of the hill too, with their mums.

Then Danny Jones came, with his dad.

And Billy Lee came, and Marcus Breen.

And then Veronique came with her mum – and her ukulele.

And that was the whole of Blue Group.

Yes!

The parents (all socially distanced) looked at each other. Then Daisy's mum frowned. 'I think we've been *organised*,' she said, and the other parents were about to agree. Before they could speak, though, Veronique told everyone to pick up a sheet of paper from the piles she'd set down on the pavement.

Which had lyrics on.

It was the wartime song Mr Ashe had mentioned: 'We'll Meet Again'. Once everyone had a copy, we all looked at Veronique.

'I'll sing it through,' she said. 'So you all know the tune.'

And she did. Or at least she started. About halfway through, though, she had to stop. There were some more people, walking down the hill. I thought Veronique was just waiting for them to go past, but they *weren't* going past. The first one was Mandy Dixon. She's in our class too, but she's in Red Group. She must have heard about what we were doing. I was about to ask her how, but I didn't get a chance; more people from our class were now walking down the hill. There was Jonathan, then Patience and Nicolo, followed by George and Aiden.

Then Martha and Tilly. Then Zoe came, with Rowan and Brooke, followed by Manon and Seraphina. In fact, EVERYONE came.

And not just from our class.

The dad with the crying Reception kid was there.

There were kids from Year One and Year Two.

Most of Year Three were there.

There were loads from Year Four and Year Five – all the years were there in fact.

And it wasn't just kids.

Mr Tucker came.

And Mrs Tompkins.

Mrs Mawford, Mrs Robinson and Mrs Luxmore. Ms Ward, Mrs Hansen, Miss de Sousa and Mrs Day. There were SO MANY people (keeping WELL apart, AND in small, separate groups) that they ranged all the way from the Stebbings's house right to the top of the hill. And, when we were sure that it was everyone, Mum – standing back from us all – got out her phone.

'Go on, Cym,' she said.

And I did. Not that I'd prepared anything. I just started to talk. I told Mrs Stebbings about our projects, and what everyone was doing. I told her about the bomb-spotters at the Valley, and Daisy's cake, and I told her all about finding Thread Street.

And I told her how much we all loved her.

Then Veronique began to play.

Do you know it – 'We'll Meet Again'? If not, you can find it online and listen. Then you'll understand. We all sang 'We'll Meet Again' for Mrs Stebbings, while Mum filmed, and I thought back to standing in the playground yesterday. This wasn't a tiny thing that I'd managed to sort out. No. It was a bit more than that, and I was so, SO proud.

Though it was NOTHING compared to what I was about to do.

With Semira's help.

Semira!

I'd got it wrong: not *everyone* in Blue Group was there. Semira wasn't, because she was at school. That she couldn't join in with the rest of us was my only regret.

Though . . .

Was she at school?

No.

Semira was coming down Morpeth Hill. Two things were different, though. The first was that she didn't have a parent with her. The second was that she wasn't walking down – she was sprinting. She had a laptop under her arm and she was weaving through all the people. And she was screaming something! I couldn't make out what, because of the singing: until she got closer. Then I could hear, and I stared.

Because Semira was screaming my name.

CHAPTER THIRTY-NINE

'CYMBELINE!'

We hadn't finished the song! I tried to ignore her and carry on singing. But I couldn't. Semira grabbed hold of my arms.

'CYMBELINE!' she bellowed.

'Semira, wait. We're . . .'

'No,' Semira said. 'I can't wait.'

'Why not? What is it?'

Seeing what was happening, Mum moved the camera away from me, towards the other people. But I was still cross. I didn't want this to be ruined. I was about to tell Semira that but, before I could, she stared into my eyes.

'Listen,' she hissed.

'All right,' I said. 'What are you doing here?'

'I ran out of school.'

It's what I'd planned to do yesterday, and here was Semira who'd actually done it. 'What? Why?'

'Because of the map!' Semira exclaimed.

A map? That's why she'd done something SO extreme – breaking out of school AND interrupting our video? I couldn't believe it, and I tried to tell her again to wait until we'd finished. Still, however, she wouldn't, though she did stop yelling at me. Instead, she opened the laptop she was holding, and held it out. An internet page popped up.

It was the London 'Bomb Sight' website.

'That's very cool,' I said. 'It is. But not now!'

Semira ignored me. 'Look!'

'At what?'

'That!' Semira squealed.

Semira pointed at the map – and I had no choice but to look at it. I saw Lewisham. I saw the river, and then what Semira was talking about: Thread Street. But I knew about that! I shook my head, about to turn away again – but I realised something.

Yesterday, Mrs Robinson had told us that Thread Street must have been knocked down after the war –

to make the DLR track. But, on the map, right next to Thread Street, there were three of those little signs: bomb symbols. So the street had been bombed. Yes, that was interesting, and I wondered if the Stebbings had still been living there then. Did they survive it in an Anderson shelter? Or had they already been evacuated? Normally I'd have been excited – but why did Semira have to tell me NOW?

'Look,' I said. 'That's interesting. But right now we're trying to . . .'

'The bombs!' Semira cried, completely not listening to me.

I sighed. 'What *about* them?'

'Look!' she insisted. She hovered over one of the symbols with the cursor, and a box popped up. Inside the box was written 'High Explosive Bomb'. I nodded because some of those were huge. It would have caused loads of damage, as would the next bomb that I could see when Semira moved the cursor. It was another high explosive bomb, and when Semira moved to the third box I wondered if it would be the same. Or would it be a V2, like the one that had hit Charlton station? Perhaps it was even an incendiary bomb.

But it wasn't.

When the third box popped up, I frowned. Inside the box, it didn't say there actually had been a bomb. It only said that there had been reports of one. There hadn't been an explosion.

'So?' I said. 'No bomb went off.'

'So think about what that means.'

'What does it mean?'

'Well, I didn't know either,' Semira said. 'So I asked Mr Amritraj. He said they're still all over London.'

'WHAT ARE?'

'Ordnance that didn't go off!'

'Ordnance?'

'Unexploded bombs!' Semira cried. 'They find more than fifty a year.'

'Now?'

'Yes. Even now. The army comes to defuse them. Unless . . .'

'Unless?'

But Semira didn't answer. She just stared at me, and I stared back into her terrified eyes until they were replaced by the image of Wansa – in the clearing where Thread Street used to be.

Bringing down the spade.

And I gasped.

All around us there was singing, the song coming to an end in a big crescendo, until that was replaced in my mind too: by the sound that I'd heard yesterday.

The crashing of metal.

On metal.

CHAPTER FORTY

I ran.

Did Mum cry out, wondering what I was doing?

I don't know. Morpeth Hill is steep and I wheeled away down it so fast that I didn't hear anything.

Soon I was at the main road.

There was nothing coming so I didn't go down to the pelican crossing. I just sprinted over, then down past my old nursery to the next road. There was traffic here and I hopped up and down outside the entrance to Silk Mills Passage, desperate to see a space. When one opened up, I dived over, seeing the troll bridge up ahead. There *were* people sitting on the steps, but I didn't care. I jumped between them, then over the bridge itself, before taking the steps on the other side three at a time. And I was there.

In Mulberry Park.

'Wansa!' I screamed.

There was no reply, of course, so I began to move again, my arms pumping as I murdered it along the path, though I didn't get far.

At the first bend, I ran straight into Meyan. She was walking towards me. She had a plastic bag in her hand and looked caught out. Was she going for more raspberries? I didn't care! It was so good to see her on this side of the river.

'Where's Wansa?' I screamed, gripping hold of Meyan's shoulders.

'What?'

'Wansa!' I repeated. 'Is she here?'

'No, she's . . .' Meyan paused and glanced behind her. I gasped and tried to get past, though Meyan wouldn't let me.

'Wait,' she said. 'You want to thank her? For the shirt?'

'Well – yes. But first . . .'

'No,' Meyan insisted. 'You can't go now.'

'But I have to.'

'In a little while. I'll go back and tell her. She'll come out to you. You need to wait a minute . . .'

'No!' I screamed. 'I can't wait.'

And I couldn't. I had to get to her. Almost having to wrestle Meyan aside, I ran on. I didn't even pause at the little wall and I didn't pause at the river. I ran straight through it – or tried to. I tripped and fell forward, water pounding into my eyes and my mouth, my right arm scraping against the tree trunk. I didn't care. I pushed myself back up and dragged myself up the far bank. I threw myself into the green tunnel, scrambling through until I emerged into the clearing.

And she was there.

'Wansa!' I panted. 'Wansa!'

But Wansa didn't hear. She was right near where she'd been yesterday, with her back to me – and she was holding the spade! When she raised her arm, lifting it up, I bellowed her name again and dived forward.

I got to her just as she dug the spade hard into the ground, the metallic *ting* singing round us as we both went tumbling over.

I don't blame her for what she did next. It was a

natural reaction. Not knowing what was happening, she scrambled back to her feet and I joined her. She began to fight me. I'd grabbed the spade. She tried to wrestle it back. I wasn't even sure that she knew it was me who'd attacked her until she stared into my face. It made no difference. Did she think I was trying to trap her? To capture her? Whatever she thought, she panicked, desperate to get the spade back until I screamed at her to STOP.

For a millisecond she did, before trying to fight again, yanking the spade until we fell backwards again, both of us nearly landing in the shallow trench that she'd been digging.

Where we stopped.

And listened.

Not to a ticking. Not like in a cartoon. It was more of a whirring sound. Like cogs. Going round.

At first, I didn't think Wansa had heard it, but she had – and she looked confused. Clearly having worked out that I wasn't there to harm her, she rolled onto her side, and pushed herself onto her knees.

And stared into the trench.

'What's that?' she said.

I didn't answer. I just listened, as the whirring sound

went on. But it was changing. It was getting a little higher in pitch.

As though the cogs were moving faster.

'Come on!' I screamed. 'WE HAVE TO GET OUT OF HERE!'

'Why? What is it? Something to do with the train track? Is it . . . ?'

'No,' I shrieked. 'It's not. I think it might be . . .'

But I didn't finish my sentence. Not right away.

Because, all of a sudden, and, without warning, a horrible silence seemed to slice through the whole clearing.

CHAPTER FORTY-ONE

As the whirring stopped.

CHAPTER FORTY-TWO

'A bomb! I think it's a bomb! A bomb from World War Two!'

Wansa's eyes and mouth jerked open. She jumped to her feet and stared into the hole again. I had the same strange impulse, but I dragged her away.

'Come on!' I bellowed, and Wansa didn't need telling again. We both hurtled across the clearing – towards the green tunnel.

But we didn't get there.

Because of Meyan.

Meyan was standing up at the mouth of the tunnel. She must have followed me. With a glance back over my shoulder I told her too – there was an unexploded bomb!

Her reaction was just as intense as Wansa's – but what she did almost knocked me over with shock. She didn't turn. She didn't dive straight back into the green tunnel.

Instead, she started forward.

I snatched hold of Meyan's wrist. I asked what she was doing but she ignored me. Instead, she spoke to Wansa, though not in English. I had no idea what she was saying, but she convinced Wansa of something. And neither of them tried to flee. They both ran past me.

Towards the tent.

'Wait!' I cried. 'Come back. Leave it. Whatever it is, it doesn't matter. It's just stuff. It doesn't matter!' I repeated, though once I'd caught up with them, I realised that it did matter.

Because it wasn't just stuff they cared about. There, lying in the open door of the tent, was the fox.

The sleeping fox!

'Rizan!' Meyan pleaded.

I figured that was the fox's name, but it gave no response. It was curled up with its snout buried into its fur. Meyan tried again and then Wansa had a go. She crawled into the tent and tried to wake up the fox. It just yawned. It thought that Wansa was playing! She tried again but it was no use and so, not even knowing what I was doing, I bent down.

And I lifted the fox up.

I did. I grabbed it round the middle and then staggered across the clearing with it as it began to stir, wriggling from my arms with a really annoyed bark. Immediately, though, Meyan grabbed it, and together we shoved it into the green tunnel. Wansa dived in after, and then Meyan pushed me in. She was last, and I could feel her behind me as we crawled madly on.

Which is when it happened.

I was moving.

I was flying forward – even before I heard the boom. It was so loud. It was almost like I was inside it, not near it. I can still feel its force as it sent me forward, though not through the green tunnel. There was no green tunnel. Instead there were bushes and brambles, thorns that ripped at my arms and face, before the ground rose up. It punched me in the side, crushing my arms against my chest until I rolled and spun. Then there was water. There were stones and mud, and all the while I saw limbs and hair, teeth and fur bowling along around me.

And the world went black.

Then it was light again.

A tree was the wrong way up. There were stones in my face, and mud. More water. I staggered to my feet, then down again – because of the ringing. It was all I could hear. I could see things. People. They were running. Screaming. A woman was there, who I recognised, holding something to her chest as she stared from across the park. Hello, Millwall baby. Then Lance's dad – was that him? Was he running towards me? Was he shouting my name? I thought so, but I couldn't hear his words.

Just the ringing sound.

Then the world went black again, though not for long.

It *was* Lance's dad. He was holding me up out of the water. I was in the river. Meyan was too. She was leaning over and coughing, Wansa still holding on to the giant fox as it started to rain.

Not raindrops.

Mud.

Clumps and dollops of earth came crashing out of the sky, along with sticks and small branches, then strips and scraps of orange as if the bomb had actually blown up the sun. It was the tent. Wansa was pointing as parts of the tent came down around us, though I still couldn't hear what she was saying. There was still just this awful ringing, which didn't stop until they got me to the hospital.

CHAPTER FORTY-THREE

I didn't see Mr Stebbings. They took me in a different way. That's when it all started to hurt. The cuts from the brambles made my face and legs feel like they were on fire. My arm – which was broken – was worse, until they gave me an injection. It made the pain dissolve, like my Weetabix fading into the milk. It was SUCH a good feeling, as was knowing Mum was there.

She'd got to Mulberry Park soon after Lance's dad, and she didn't leave me. You'll have to take her word for what happened next. I don't remember it. She told me in the days that followed.

I was in the operating theatre. They were going to operate on my arm. Apparently, just before the anaesthetic put me out, I said I had something to say.

I was desperate, and even struggled to prop myself upright.

'Cym?' Mum asked. 'What is it, love?'

'Is it okay? Mum?'

Mum didn't know what I was talking about. 'Cymbeline?'

'You know,' I mumbled, and Mum took hold of my good hand.

'You mean that fox? That those girls had?'

'No. I saw the fox. I know it's fine.'

'Then . . . ?'

'There's only one,' I insisted.

'One what?'

'Brett Casey. He's gone to Wycombe Wanderers. So it's unique. Is my shirt OKAY, Mum?'

CHAPTER FORTY-FOUR

I was in hospital for nearly a month. It was my arm. I'd managed to break it in a really complicated way. They put it in this huge cast that made me look like I was trying to ask a question all the time. It was so boring – apart from the pain. I had to have stitches in my leg and face and then have those stitches out. Not nice. Then I had to have another operation on my arm. I spent the days longing for visitors – only Mum was allowed in – and trying to guess which nurse was which because of all the protective stuff they still had to wear. Apart from that, I watched stuff on Mum's tablet and listened to audiobooks, though I found it hard to concentrate. I kept thinking of Wansa and Meyan.

'Where are they?' I asked after two days. I'd told Mum all about them by now. She said that they had been in hospital but with only minor injuries. They were out now but she didn't know where they'd been taken. She was trying to find out. A charity had seen what had happened – on the news – and was going to help them.

'And Jackie Chapman's helping too.'

'What?'

'He saw the news as well. He recognised your name. He's set up a fund to raise money. He's put it on social media.'

'Like Marcus Rashford?'

Mum smiled and I nodded to myself. It's why I wanted to be a footballer – so I could help people. Not that I'd be able to practise for AGES.

'Will I be okay for next season?' I asked Mum. 'For when the league starts up again?'

Mum said she hoped that I would be, and then leant in for a whisper. 'I saw you, you know?'

'Do what?'

'The Super Seven. In the park that time. Cross my heart.' Mum winked at me. 'But what you just did is far more impressive. You know that, don't you?'

I nodded, and thought of Mulberry Park, and knew that I should have felt proud. But I was worried about Wansa and Meyan, and most of all, I was afraid.

'How's Mrs Stebbings?' I said.

The answer to that was the same. She was in the ICU.

'But have they shown her the video?'

Mum said yes, or at least they'd tried to. Mrs Stebbings's nurses played it to her a lot, though they weren't sure if she could hear it.

'She can,' I insisted. 'I know she can.' And I begged Mum to keep me updated.

Meanwhile I read the news on her tablet and was amazed at how many people were ill with coronavirus. And how many people were dying from it. But Mrs Stebbings wasn't going to be one of them!

I asked about her every day, though it wasn't until I was back at home that I found out the truth. Mum and I were in the kitchen. Mum had called me through to show me something she was cooking. She took it out of the oven and set it on a cooling tray: something thin, circular and very, very hard.

'Is that . . . ?' I started.

'What?'

'I dunno.' I rubbed my chin. 'A bake-your-own Frisbee?'

'Cymbeline! It's bread.'

'Bread?'

'It's called sourdough. I'm not sure I did it right. Though this is good. Here.'

Mum held a pan out to me that held brown, gloopy stuff. I sniffed it and Mum sighed.

'Go on. It won't hurt you. Home-made chocolate spread. No palm oil in that!'

And I did try it and it was amazing. It would probably even make the sourdough taste good. Mum was trying to cut some when the doorbell went. She walked through to answer it and then I hurried through after her.

Because I could see Mr Stebbings.

He was standing back from our door. He had his suit on. He was looking very serious, and when I reached Mum, she took hold of my good arm and held it.

'Albert?' she said. 'Is . . . ?'

Mum's voice trailed away and I saw her swallow. Then we both stared, but Mr Stebbings didn't answer. He had a phone in his hand, and he looked at it for a second before holding it out towards us.

'A video,' he said. 'The nurse sent me it just now. I was outside the hospital but I came here straight away. I wanted you to be the first to see it.'

And what I saw was a tiny woman, surrounded by wires and tubes and machines.

But who was holding one of her thumbs up.

'She's going to be all right,' Mr Stebbings said, a grin cracking his whole face open.

And, in spite of the fact that it was SO painful, I jumped up and down with joy.

CHAPTER FORTY-FIVE

We chatted for a bit and then I left Mum and Mr Stebbings at the door. I went back inside and collapsed – on the Seated Optimal Flop-out Activator.

Then I thought about lockdown. I'd assumed that it would shut my life down but, instead, it had sent me on an incredible journey. I'd found Wansa and Meyan. I'd found Semira. I'd discovered a whole school full of people who cared about one of their own.

And it wasn't just me. Mum had been on a journey too. She'd gone from scared and anxious, to understanding that, if we all did everything that we could, then we stood a good chance of getting through this. She'd understood that it was okay to be scared, and we'd BOTH realised just how much we cared for Stephan, Mabel and Ellen. And how much we missed having them in our lives, which made me have another thought.

I knew that coronavirus and lockdown were awful things. That they hurt so many people. But I couldn't see how these last weeks hadn't been good for us, in spite of how bashed up I was. I'd made new friends. I'd saved some of those friends from a bomb – and Mrs Stebbings was okay! We were so lucky. It almost felt like we'd completely escaped coronavirus, that none of the really bad things had got close to us.

And then things got even better.

First, I had my cast off. It happened three days after Mr Stebbings came round – and my arm was perfect. I'd have to steer away from any kind of football for another three months, but so what? I'd get back to it soon enough. I *would* get back to normal. I was SO relieved, and then more so. Mum took a phone call and looked so delighted that I hopped up and down with impatience until she'd finished.

'Was that . . . ?'

'The charity,' she said. 'Yes.'

'And?'

'Wansa and Meyan will have to plead their case to

stay here but the charity thinks they'll win. It won't be for a while, though.'

'Then what will they do in the meantime?'

'They'll be under the care of the local authority.'

'What?'

'In a sort of children's home. But they won't be there for much longer. They can come out if . . .'

'What?'

'Well, Meyan is actually an adult now, so she is Wansa's legal guardian. That means they won't need an official foster home.'

'What will they need?'

'A place to live. Somewhere stable and with people who will guarantee their presence. That's it.'

'So . . . Mum!' I screamed. 'They can . . . ?'

'Stay here? Yes.'

'That's incredible. Can Wansa come to our school? She could be on the football team. She's fantastic.'

'I'll ask. But it'll take some rejigging. You'll have to move next door, though, just to sleep.'

'Next door? You mean with . . . ?'

'Stephan, Mabel and Ellen.'

'What?' I bellowed, which is when Mum told me that they were all coming back.

'Because of this?'

'In a way. When I told Stephan, he did want to help. But it's the girls. They love it over there, but they grew up here. It's rainy and cramped and we might not have their great government. But this is their home. They're already on their way. They just have to quarantine for a bit longer.'

And, once again, I jumped up and down with joy.

I did that for the next three days as we got ourselves ready. Mum packed up my things and took a lot of them next door. I got Mabel's unicorn drawings out from under my bed, and put them all back up.

When the doorbell went again, I answered it.

And Mabel came flying into my legs.

And Stephan came flying into Mum's arms.

And we all came back inside – which is where I wish I could stop this story.

Where I wish I could write 'The End'.

But I can't.

Because it goes on, like the river in Mulberry Park.

Whether I want it to or not.

You see, we hadn't escaped coronavirus after all.

EPILOGUE

Mum woke me up a bit early. I was still in our house. Meyan and Wansa hadn't got there yet. I ate breakfast and got dressed, my arm playing up a bit. Mum gave me some Calpol and put it in a sling so that everyone else would know not to be rough with me. That took a little while, though we did leave on time.

For school.

Because lockdown – at least for schools – was over.

We weren't late leaving, but we did have a problem. Mum only uses the car to go to work, really, and she hadn't been there for ages. The battery was flat. Stephan gave us a jump-start from his car, but we still had to get a move on or Mum would be late for work. There was quite a lot of traffic about because of schools going back, and when we got to the top of the steps that lead down to our school, Mum wanted me just to hop out.

I was happy to, but Mum's phone pinged from inside her bag. She turned the engine off, read a text, and frowned.

'What is it?' I said.

Mum told me that the school wanted parents to come into the playground that morning, with their kids. I asked why, but Mum shrugged, so we got out, immediately seeing Vi and her dad, who'd just walked across Blackheath. Vi's dad was putting his phone back into his coat pocket and he and Mum looked at each other. They then looked around at the other parents, who were all, now, converging on the school. It was obvious that no one knew what was happening, though, and so we all walked down the steps and then through the gates, more parents, and some of the kids, shrugging at each other. Mr Amritraj was there – standing back from the gate, directing people through. We all wanted to ask him what was going on but Mr Amritraj's gaze was fixed high above our heads, his lips pressed together, his fists clenched at his sides. It was weird. And scary.

Because it looked like he'd been crying.

And he wasn't the only one.

Once we all got into the playground, I looked around for the teachers so that us kids could line up. The teachers weren't ranged along the back wall though. Instead, they were positioned round the edges of the playground, a small group gathered at the far end, near the wooden stage. The first one I saw was Mrs Robinson, and seeing her stopped me.

Mrs Robinson was batting her hands at her face, her mouth making a little 'O'. Miss Phillips was next to her. She was holding one of her elbows, her other hand pressed into her face. Both of her arms were shaking. They stayed shaking as Mr Tucker came up and put his arms around her, which made me stare: tears were streaming down the side of his face into his shirt collar.

'Mum?' I said.

But Mum didn't answer. She just put her arm round my shoulder and drew me to her, other parents doing the same with their kids, all with space around them. I began to get this hollow feeling in my stomach, which got worse when my eyes fell on Mrs Martin. Our head teacher.

Mrs Martin was walking through to us from the staff room. We all made space for her as she headed across the playground towards the stage, though she didn't go up the steps at first. Instead, she stood, with her back to us, taking deep breaths until she stumbled to the side, Mr Tucker and Mrs Robinson rushing forward to steady her. They then held on to her, supporting her as she climbed the steps, and they kept doing that as Mrs Martin turned round to face us all. Like Mr Amritraj, she had her lips pressed together, her face so struck with pain that it made us all go silent. Then her eyes flitted around the playground – to take us all in – as my eyes went to her left hand.

In it was the school phone.

I swallowed. Then I clenched my fists, as Mrs Martin's mouth opened, and then closed. She was trying to force herself to speak, though I didn't want her to. No.

No.

I didn't want her to say it – because it couldn't be. I'd seen that video – and not only that. I'd seen Mrs Stebbings! I'd gone round to her house. Twice. The first time, she'd only been able to wave from the window, but the second time she'd come out. And she'd thanked me – *so* much. She'd told me to thank everyone else – and she'd sworn that she was fine.

So . . .

What had happened?

A relapse?

Had it all happened suddenly?

It must have, but there was something strange, something I couldn't work out until I realised.

There *was* Mrs Stebbings.

I'd walked past her. Mrs Stebbings was standing by the hall door and when I spun round I saw that she was still standing there – staring at us all with tears streaming down her face too.

So?

I turned away from Mrs Stebbings. Then I spun round. I saw Mrs Tompkins. She was near the climbing wall. I saw Mrs Luxmore. I saw Ms Ward and Mrs Hansen. No. Please. I saw Mr Gibbs. I saw Mrs Mawford with her hands clasped together. I saw Miss Phillips and Mrs Robinson again, and I saw Mrs Day. No. No. No. No. No.

And I turned this way and that, until my eyes happened to fall on Vi. And her face. It was awful. She'd been looking round too, and so had Daisy, next to her. Lance was doing the same thing, and Billy, all looking so scared. I wanted to be with Vi so I slipped away from Mum and went up to her. Billy moved away from his mum, and then Lance moved away from his dad. Marcus Breen and Danny Jones came up. Veronique came and then more of us, all the parents letting us go and all the other year groups making way – until we were together. Our class. We were all there in the middle of the playground as we all started to take each other's hands. I don't know whose I took. I didn't care. I just knew I was holding my classmates' hands as we all bunched up together and carried on looking round, each of us desperate.

To see one face.

The face of the person who was at the centre of us all.

Our football coach.

Our teacher.

Our best friend, who we all shared, in spite of who our other best friends might be.

Mr Ashe.

EPILOGUE TWO

He hadn't wanted to worry us.

Mrs Robinson told us that.

We had her a week later, when we went back. When he'd got ill, the first thing Mr Ashe had made the school promise was that none of us would have to worry about him. That's why they'd told us he was on a course. The words made us all go silent as each and every one of us had the same thought. We all knew that Mr Ashe had cared for us.

But we never knew how much.

Not ever.

Mrs Robinson read us a letter: from Mr Ashe. In it, he told us all that we had to carry on. That we had to play, and support each other, and make the most of life, and never, ever forget our fronted adverbials. That made us laugh but then we quietened down again as he mentioned each and every one of us by name. A lot of people cried when Mrs Robinson got to their name, and I was one of them. Hearing my name just made me feel so special – knowing that Mr Ashe had thought of me. When Mrs Robinson finished there was silence, until Semira put her hand up.

'Can we sing, please?' she asked.

And we did sing. We sang 'We'll Meet Again'. Halfway through, the door opened and a figure stood there, a thinner figure than before but still there nonetheless.

Mrs Stebbings.

And she joined in the singing too.

And that is the end – apart from this.

For lunch that day we had the STP. It was amazing, but it tasted different. And it still does, every time I have it. It tastes far better because, for some reason, it makes me think of Mr Ashe.

As does my shirt.

My Charlton shirt, which Mum held out to me when she picked me up that day.

Mum hadn't been teaching at her school, so she didn't

have the car. We walked across the heath, but not towards home. We went down towards Lewisham, then past the train station. We carried on towards Lee and then stopped: at the framer's. There was a queue outside because they were only letting one person in at a time, and while we stood in it, I held the shirt out. Mum had done a great job. The shirt had been full of holes. After I got sent through the brambles it was torn, and tattered, with a huge slit in the side because the paramedics had had to cut it off me to get to my arm. But Mum had mended it, after which I'd tried to give it to Mrs Stebbings. She wouldn't take it. She said it was far too precious. She told me to hang it back up on my bedroom wall in a frame, which is why we were there.

But, suddenly, it all seemed very clear: I wasn't going to do that.

No.

'What is it, Cym?' Mum said, when I stepped to the side of the queue.

I didn't answer. I just smiled, and heard Mrs Robinson's voice, as she read out Mr Ashe's letter.

'Make the most of life.'

So I took Mum's hand, led her away from the shop, and put the shirt on.

EPILOGUE THREE

P.S. I knitted Mrs Stebbings a Charlton scarf instead. It was cable knit, and that's HARD.

It took me **AGES.**

THE END

ACKNOWLEDGEMENTS

First I have to thank the four people who I'm lucky enough to live with for keeping me sane during the pandemic: Naomi, Franklin, Viola and Frieda. I couldn't have asked for a better crew to be locked up with. Your comments on the story as it went along, and all your ideas, were invaluable. I have great editors in Nick Lake and Julia Sanderson: thanks for helping me knock the block into better shape. Thanks also to Leena Lane for the final fine-tuning. Thanks, as ever, to the wonderful Jessica Dean and all the publicity folk at HarperCollins, who send me out to schools and festivals during the year. It's so wonderful to meet my readers, young and old. Thanks also to all at Authors Aloud. I can honestly say that I've never been received with anything less than warmth and enthusiasm on my visits, so a massive thanks to all the librarians and teachers who I've met and have yet to meet. You are in inspiration. I also have a wonderful agent in Cathryn Summerhayes – thanks C, and all at Curtis Brown. When's the next party?

I hope it's not too selfish to thank the teachers who were brilliant at getting my own children through the pandemic. If you work at All Saints, Greycoats or St Olaves, then you are wonderful. Finally I'd like to thank you, the reader. The pandemic was hard on all of us, but for some it was much, much worse. If you are one of these people, I hope I've represented our collective experience in a way that is sensitive and meaningful to you.

TURN OVER TO READ MORE ABOUT THE FUNNY AND HEARTWARMING BOOKS WRITTEN BY CRITICALLY ACCLAIMED AUTHOR ADAM BARON . . .

Selected as Waterstones Book of the Month and shortlisted for the Carnegie Medal, *Boy Underwater* is a heartbreaking story about family, friends and secrets. And it's very, very funny.

Cymbeline (yes, really!) has never been swimming – not ever, not once – so he's a bit nervous at the prospect of his first school swimming lesson ever. But how hard could it be? He's Googled front crawl, and he's found his dad's old pair of trunks. He's totally ready for this.

But he's not ready for an accident at the pool to reveal a family mystery that turns his life completely upside down. Only Cym and his friends can solve it because, as usual, the grown-ups aren't telling them anything.

For the answers you really need, sometimes you have to go deep . . .

From the author of bestselling debut *Boy Underwater* comes another moving, hilarious novel of friendship and family secrets, which shows that people are people, no matter where they're from.

Here's something you won't believe: someone is doing TERRIBLE things to Mrs Martin, Cymbeline Igloo's favourite teacher of all time.

Cymbeline has to find the culprit (after he's learned what 'culprit' means). He's also got to help his friend Veronique, whose grandma is dangerously ill. It seems Nanai has a secret, connected to her arrival in the UK as a Boat Person from Vietnam, a traumatic journey in which she lost her twin sister. Can Cymbeline figure out the mystery in time?

One thing is for sure: even the most unexpected people can change your life in wonderful ways . . .

***This Wonderful Thing* is a moving and hilarious novel about friendships, family secrets, mystery – and life-changing hidden treasure . . .**

Jessica is playing with her family at the river when she finds a dirty, bedraggled teddy bear in the water.

She has no idea that it will change everything, forever.

Meanwhile, Cymbeline comes home from school to find that his mum's house has been broken into – and the thieves seemed oddly focused on his toys. Thank goodness he had Not Mr Fluffy, his Bear of Most Extreme Importance, with him.

Soon, Jessica and Cymbeline find themselves swept up in a mystery that spans decades, threatens their families and turns their lives upside down.

But sometimes, just maybe, a new life can be a really wonderful thing . . .